THE PAWN

CATHERINE BANKS

TURBO KITTEN

The Pawn by Catherine Banks

Turbo Kitten Industries™

P.O. Box 5012, Galt, CA 95632

www.turbokitten.us

Catherine Banks www.catherinebanks.com

❀ Created with Vellum

Chapter 1

I woke to Apollo's shouts as he rode his chariot across the sky, pulling the sun behind him. Morning always came too soon for me.

"Wake up sleepy girls! Time to get up!" Apollo shouted as he passed over us. "Achillia! I know you're still lying in bed. Get up lazy girl."

I groaned in embarrassment. Why did he have to single me out? I rolled out of bed and grumbled, "Thank you, Apollo for announcing my laziness to everyone."

Apollo laughed loudly, which made me smile in spite of his rudeness. His laugh always made me smile, but then again, it was hard to stay angry with a god when he was happy.

After dressing and finishing my morning customs, I walked out of my room and into the chaos of the House of Eros. Eros had ten servants, five women and five men and I was one of the lucky women who got to serve him. We were each given duties, which we are required to perform each day and a break at the end of the day when we finish all of the duties. I always finished early so I had more time to myself, but lately I'd been having more training sessions with Ares, God of War and Eros' father, and less time to myself.

I walked quickly through the halls to the main dining room and stepped inside, taking a deep breath for courage. Eros sat on his throne, watching the servants whose job it was to bring the food to the giant table where we all ate. A woman stood on each side of him, fanning and ogling him openly. He was handsome with his father's strong, masculine jaw and his mother, Aphrodite's, beautiful blue eyes and luscious blonde curls. He could make any mortal swoon and happened to be the God of Love.

I often had to reprimand myself from becoming like the crazy, stalker-type, obsessed women who served him, two of whom were currently fanning him.

Eros noticed me waiting beside the entranceway and smiled. "Achillia, I see you're finally out of bed. Was Apollo's announcement loud enough?"

I blushed and looked down at the marble beneath my feet. "I apologize, Great Eros. I shall not be so lazy again." Even though I tried for submissive and apologetic, the ending came out angry and obstinate.

Eros laughed despite my tone and motioned me forward. I walked slowly towards him, breathing deeply and evenly.

He was only a god. A handsome, breathtaking, hunk of a god. But still, only one god out of many. He was not even the best-looking god. You can behave and not act like a mortal driven by hormones for ten minutes.

I looked up when I got to the base of his throne and smiled. "Yes, Eros?"

He put his hands out and the girls stopped fanning him, glaring at me for taking his attention away. I fought the urge to make an obscene gesture at them and looked at Eros as he addressed me. "My father says you're doing well in your lessons."

Ares told him about my lessons?

"He said you're the most advanced of the women here."

Well the others were too afraid to break a nail or damage their good looks and ruin a chance at being with Eros to take fighting seriously.

"If you keep up the good work you might be promoted."

I stared at him, eyes wide. "Promoted? Promotion is an option?" I'd always thought you were just assigned a position and forced to stay there.

Eros looked as though he wanted to continue, but Ares chose that moment to walk in the room. Eros rushed to stand, the other servants and I turned and dropped to the floor, bowing with our foreheads touching the cool marble beneath us just as quickly. Ares walked past the groveling servants until his feet stopped before my hands. I stared in surprise at the closeness of them. "Eros, I need to train more with Achillia."

Eros cleared his throat before answering. "Of course, Father. I'm sure she would be more than willing to work faster on her chores or..."

"No," Ares cut Eros off, "I want you to reassign her chores to someone else. I want her time specifically for training with me."

No chores? Only training with Ares? Could Zeus give me any more blessings?

Eros fought a moment for composure. I could hear him rustling around before he finally spoke. "I don't think I can spare her from—"

Ares' anger was quick, and his tone was short. "You will

find a way to spare her! This is not a request, but a command. Do we have an understanding?"

"Of course, Father. I did not mean to offend you," Eros said softly.

Ares sighed. "No, of course you didn't. You never mean to offend anyone."

I stifled a laugh and pressed my forehead harder into the ground.

"Achillia."

I answered without looking up. "Yes, Great Ares?"

"Stand up, girl. I hate talking to you while you're lying on the ground." I stood up and smoothed down my short, white, knee-length tunic, the longest tunic worn by any of Eros' female servants, and looked up at Ares. He smiled and it took me a minute to remember how to breathe. Where Eros was handsome and angelic, Ares was masculine and dangerous. Women wanted him for a whole other reason why they wanted Eros. The god of war waited while my mortal brain relaxed from the initial shock of seeing him and then he smiled. "Have you eaten?"

My eyes were drawn to the table, but stopped them at the last second. "No."

He nodded as if he knew the answer already. No surprise, he could see the servants still placing food on the table. "I'll feed you when we get there. Come. It's time to intensify your training."

Intensify? That didn't sound pleasurable.

Eros watched Ares leave, his eyes glued to the back of Ares' head in an angry glare. I followed after, but I spared one more look at Eros when I reached the entranceway and found him staring at me now, a look of want and jealousy marring his perfect features. It was a look I'd never before seen on a god's face and it frightened me.

I followed Ares silently out of the house and into the open. What could he do to intensify my training? Would he make me climb Mount Olympus? Would he make me fight a Cyclops?

Ares stopped walking when he reached the edge of the grass field he used as his training ground and turned to me. "You are forbidden to repeat anything I say from this point forward. You understand?"

I nodded and focused on breathing, or I worried I might forget to. "Those other girls, are useless. The only things they're good for are cleaning, cooking, and pleasure. You, on the other hand, are exactly what I was hoping for when I had Eros make you."

The gods made all of their servants from the bones of dead mortals. We were even given names to represent our origin. I was made from the bones of the late Achilles, the hero of the Trojan War and one of the greatest warriors ever. That's why I was called "Achillia," which meant "daughter of Achilles."

I had never known that Ares had commanded Eros to make me though. Why would he have Eros make me? I frowned.

Ares snapped his fingers and a wooden bench appeared behind me. I sat down and smiled in thanks at him. He snapped his fingers again and his throne, which was made of bones from the great kings he had conquered, appeared behind him. He sat down and a table with fresh fruit, cheese, bread, and wine appeared between us. I started eating from the table while he talked.

"Yes, I had you made from Achilles' bones. I needed a warrior among Eros' women. I was hoping you might even pique his interest in other ways, but he's much like his mother in the fact that they are both easily distracted."

I squeezed my lips together to keep from laughing, which made Ares lift a brow at me. He smiled and relaxed into his chair. "Eros did well when he made you. You're exactly what I wanted. You've heard about the decline of our Messordei?"

That was quite a topic shift. And who hadn't heard about the Messordei problem? The Messordei, or "reapers of the gods," were warriors completely loyal to the god who created them. The Messordei had been mainly fighting with the warlocks of the mortal world and sadly, losing. We started off with sixty Messordei and now we were down to twenty. It was making the gods look bad in the mortal realm.

"Yes, I've heard about it," I answered.

He exhaled and rubbed his temples. "Athena and I have been arguing for weeks about the proper course of action. She has given me one chance to prove my plan will work." He looked up at me and smiled. "So, let's get to work. I have a lot to teach you and not much time."

Did he mean I was his last chance to prove his plan? Surely he couldn't think I could help them in anyway? "I don't think—"

Ares arched an eyebrow at me and the look stopped the words from coming out. "You will be tested today and train excruciatingly hard every day after until I'm sure that you are indeed ready."

Ready for what?

Ares stood from his throne and it disappeared instantly. I stood and the bench behind me and the table disappeared as well. Ares led the way through the grassy area towards a canyon where Eros spent time meditating. It felt wrong to be going to the canyon, since Eros had forbade us from ever going there. I stood at the entrance to the canyon and swallowed nervously. One more step and I'd have crossed the border into Eros' private area. One more step and I would be breaking one of the biggest rules Eros had ever made. One more step and...

Someone shoved me from behind, forcing me to stumble three steps forward and into the canyon. I crouched down and cringed, waiting for Eros' wrath.

Nothing happened.

I stood up and found Ares frowning at me. "Did you think I would lead you into a place where you would get hurt?"

I blushed and looked at the ground. "No. I just—"

Ares sighed. "Forget it. I'm tired of politics. Come Achillia, let's get to your lesson."

I snuck a glance behind me to see who had pushed me, but there was no one there. Strange.

I followed Ares farther into the canyon, my heart pounding harder with each step until all I could hear was its beating. Ares was talking and stopped next to a small rock a few yards ahead. I walked quicker to catch what he was saying when I realized he wasn't talking to me. Heracles stood in front of Ares, and I knew then that my training had indeed intensified. Heracles was tall, at least six foot seven, with biceps as big as my head and legs that looked like they could move a mountain. Ares turned around and waved me forward. "Achillia meet Heracles."

I walked until I was standing beside Ares and curtsied. "Hello, sir."

Heracles looked from Ares to me and then back again. "Her? She doesn't look the part, Ares."

My jaw clenched at the disdain in his voice. "Does my appearance bother you, sir?" I knew I should have been more respectful, but I hated it when people assumed I was just a pretty, dumb girl like the other girls Eros made.

Ares was smiling broadly as Heracles turned to frown at me. "You are small, fragile, and exceptionally female. You are also too pretty to have any chance as a fighter. Ares, how could you even think one of Eros' girls could possibly meet your expectations?"

Did he really think I was that pretty? *Focus.* I growled at myself as I pushed the other thoughts to the side. "Just because I'm a woman from the House of Eros does not mean I am like the rest of the simple-minded morons who swoon over Eros. I may be small and female, but I am not fragile and I have a much better chance at being a fighter than anyone else."

Ares was smiling so wide now I thought his face might split. "Heracles, why don't you test her skills out? See if she's as fragile as you think?"

Heracles glared at Ares. "You know I don't hit defenseless women."

That did it! Now he was going to pay! Before I could think logically about what I was doing, I'd crossed the distance between Heracles and me and hit him in the jaw. He stumbled backwards and stared at me, his eyes as wide as the full moon.

Heracles glared at Ares and then walked towards me. "I don't want to hit you."

I looked back at Ares. "What do you want me to do? If he doesn't want to fight and personally I'd rather not fight Heracles what should I do?"

Ares sat on the top of the rock he had been standing beside and said, "Here's the situation you are both going to pretend you're in. I, the great God Ares, have been injured and am unable to defend myself. You, Achillia, must protect me from Heracles who wishes to kill his poor wounded Uncle Ares."

Heracles rolled his eyes, but turned back to me. "I'm not going to go full force. I promise if I land a punch that it won't hurt."

I smiled. "Sorry, but I can't say the same for you. I have a duty and obligation to protect Ares, God of War."

Heracles stared at me for a moment before trying to rush around me and get to Ares. I dropped down and swung my legs out, knocking Heracles' legs out from under him. He landed on his back, but instantly jumped up. I ran forward and started attacking him, but he blocked all of my punches. I was successfully pushing him backwards, away from Ares, though.

Heracles noticed our slow retreat and ground his teeth together before switching from defensive to offensive. I ducked his first wild swing and got him in the stomach with an upper cut. He grunted and tried to grab me, but I rolled underneath him and between his legs. I turned to kick him, but he'd already spun around and seized my leg. I started to prepare myself to kick him with my other leg, but he dropped the leg he held and took a step back, towards Ares. I moved forward, kicking and hitting him, but my assault was pushing him towards Ares still. I grunted and swung around him to kick him in the back and push him away from the poor defenseless god who was watching our fight intently.

Heracles grabbed me in a bear hug and squeezed the breath from my lungs. "Give up," he whispered in my ear.

I stomped on the inside of his foot and growled, "Never!"

His arms dropped from around me, and I elbowed him in the side before spinning away to kick him in the chest. He flew backwards and landed on his rump in the dirt at least ten yards away.

I brushed off my tunic and took the ready stance Ares had taught me. Heracles stood and brushed off his rump before glaring at me. "Alright, I'm done going easy on you."

I smiled. "Alright, then I'll stop going easy on you, too."

He growled loudly, sounding like a lion and looking every bit as magnificent as his father, Zeus, and rushed forward. I thought he had been fast before, but now I could see his demigod speed. He grabbed ahold of my shoulders and tried to run me back towards Ares. I couldn't let that happen. I couldn't let him get to Ares. I grabbed his hands and propelled myself up and over him, landing on his back and wrapped my arm around his throat. I held on tightly as he slapped at me and tried to dislodge me.

I would not lose. I could not lose. I had to protect Ares.

Heracles' face turned red and then the color began draining from his face. I held on as he dropped to his knees and then to the ground. Out cold.

I released my hold and stared in utter disbelief at the unconscious demigod. I'd just choked out Heracles. *The* Heracles! Oh no! He was never going to forgive me. I'd just made my first enemy.

I backed away quickly and would have run away if Ares hadn't grabbed my shoulder. "Relax, Achillia." I relaxed in his touch and forced my hormones at bay. Ares held me at arm's length and smiled. "You did incredibly well. Better than I thought you would. I'm very pleased."

I blushed and looked away from him. Heracles groaned at our feet as he started to wake up. Ares picked me up and gently set me on the top of the rock where he had previously been sitting. I folded my legs beneath me and tugged my tunic down to cover my knees. I could be demure when necessary and right now I desperately needed to be demure so as not to upset Heracles anymore than I already had.

Ares helped Heracles stand and patted him on the back. "I told you."

Heracles shook his head then grinned at Ares. "Yeah, well I wouldn't have believed it, if I hadn't experienced it." Heracles turned to me and his smile turned from happy to seductive. "I have to admit, you're incredible."

I swallowed and whispered, "Thank you."

Ares looked back at Heracles. "You think she's ready?"

Heracles nodded. "Yes, but I think you might try her against another first."

Another? They wanted me to fight someone else? Oh gods, who else could they have me fight? Who was more of a test than Heracles?

Ares seemed to be thinking the same thing. "Who do you suggest?"

"Artemis."

Ares and I stared at Heracles in complete shock. Artemis? The goddess of the hunt? Surely, he couldn't think I could win against a goddess like that. Especially, when she used a bow and I had no weapon?

Ares stroked his goatee in thought for a moment and then nodded. "Yes, that would be a good test. I could train her in a form of weaponry and then try her against Artemis. That would be the ultimate test."

"Or you could try her against me," said an all-too-familiar male voice.

I didn't bother to turn around because I knew he would approach me. I sat perfectly still as the warmth of a perfect summer day surrounded me. The scent of spring rain on pines and of a field of summer flowers surrounding me made me exhale as my body relaxed. I closed my eyes and enjoyed the warmth, and then opened them to find Apollo standing in front of me.

"Hello, Achillia."

I smiled at the golden-haired god of the sun and bowed my head. "Apollo."

Heracles raised an eyebrow and looked at Ares and then Apollo. "She seems to know quite a few gods."

I blushed and looked down at my hands, which were now clenched in my lap. It wasn't my fault that many of the male gods visited Eros and asked for his servants. Sure I was acquainted with many of the gods, but I'd never done anything with any of them. Eros was extremely strict on that part when anyone asked for my company.

Ares glared at Heracles. "Do not insult this girl's virtue. Apologize."

Heracles looked from me to Ares to Apollo and then back to me. "You're truly untouched?" I nodded. He sighed. "Then I apologize. I should not have made assumptions."

I shrugged. "I accept your apology and I understand. Eros' women are known for their...talents, which we gain from Eros. Fortunately, I was made from Achilles and not a love struck mortal like the other women."

Apollo looked at Ares. "You had her made from Achilles' bones? How is that possible? She's...well she's a woman."

Ares smiled. "You can use the bones of either gender. The gender of the prior person's bones does not determine the gender of the person being made. The maker determines the gender."

Apollo rubbed his chin. "Well, that's useful information. I wasn't aware of that."

Ares folded his arms across his chest and asked, "And who did you think she was made from with the name of 'Achillia'?"

Apollo shrugged. "I presumed she was made from a woman of Achilles' line, not Achilles himself."

"Well that's why you shouldn't presume things," I answered in a cheery voice.

Apollo rolled his eyes at me, used to my teasing, and turned back to Ares. "Teach her to use a weapon, and I will test her."

Heracles looked at Ares. "Artemis would be a better test."

Apollo's skin began glowing as the power of the sun began to seep out. "Are you insulting me?"

Heracles stood tall and strong and smiled. "Feeling inadequate?"

I couldn't believe it. Heracles was taunting a god. I taunted gods, but only because as a woman I could get away with a lot and I usually only taunted gods that I had a friendly relationship with. Taunting a god you had no such relationship with was never a smart idea.

Ares sighed and stepped between them. "Let's focus on the main issue here, gentlemen. Over the next two days I'll teach Achillia to use one weapon and then Apollo will test her. If she's not ready by then, my plan will have failed."

I blinked at Ares. Great. No pressure on me. I still didn't understand what he thought I could do for him. It's not like I could create more Messordei or defeat all of the warlocks that the Messordei couldn't. I was just a god's servant, not a warrior or fighter.

Heracles turned away from Apollo and to Ares. "You mind sending me back now?"

Apollo smiled. "Still can't figure out how to travel with the new powers?"

New powers? I looked at Heracles, and my breath caught in my throat. That's what was different about him. He was immortal now. I hadn't heard that he'd finally finished his quest for immortality and joined the gods.

Heracles ignored Apollo's taunt and instead turned to me. He walked forward and picked up my hand, gently kissing the back of it. "It was a pleasure meeting you, Achillia. I hope I might get a chance to spar with you again sometime."

I put on my best, sweetest smile and said, "The pleasure was mine and I look forward to sparring with you again in the future."

Ares touched Heracles on the shoulder, and he disappeared. I relaxed, only to find Ares and Apollo watching me. "What?"

Apollo shook his head. "Nothing. Ares, I'll see you in two days." Apollo took one last look at me, sadness and something that looked vaguely like jealousy twisting his features, and then he disappeared in a ray of sunshine.

I turned to Ares and asked, "What in the Underworld is going on? What did I do to upset Apollo?"

Ares rubbed his temples a moment before looking at me. "You don't understand the effect you have, do you?"

I frowned at him. "What do you mean? What effect?"

Ares helped me climb down from the rock and started walking back out of the canyon. "As one of Eros' servants you have learned the ways of…" Ares stopped and turned to face me. "I had you made from a warrior's bones, and I hope you have the heart of one. Can you take some helpful insights from me?"

I nodded, and bit my bottom lip.

He sighed and walking again. "You were trained by Eros to be beautiful, seductive, and flirtatious. You have that down superbly. However, you are also strong, independent, and caring. Those are attributes none of the other servants have. Those are attributes that men look for in the women they choose as wives." He stopped again and looked at me.

Now I understood. Because I wasn't the bubbly, easy-to-sleep-with girl, and because of my warrior qualities, I was considered wife material. And until now, I hadn't realized that every god who visited me often wasn't just visiting me for friendship, he was courting me, trying to convince me to be his wife. Which was why Apollo had been jealous and sad when he saw me flirt with Heracles. Oh, Zeus! What was I going to do?

Ares put a hand out to steady me as I swayed on my feet. "Achillia?"

I pulled away from his hand and exhaled. "I'm fine. Just… wow." I looked up at Ares and asked, "You're not? I mean, you aren't one of the—"

Ares smiled and shook his head. "No, Achillia. You're my creation, like a daughter to me, and I love you as such."

I exhaled and relaxed against the wall of the canyon. "No offense, Ares, but that's a great relief to me."

Ares laughed. "You're lucky I know what you mean and I don't take that for what it could mean. Now, we need to get back and figure out what weapon to train you with."

We walked in silence until we reached the training area. I sat down on the bench Ares produced for me and waited while he conferred with Hephaistos, who had appeared as soon as I sat down. Hephaistos brought out a bow and arrow and handed them to me. I held the weapons as Ares instructed, but as soon as I let the string go, the arrow flew past the target at the end of the field. Hephaistos sighed and took the bow from me. He tapped his chin for a minute and then produced a spear. I tested the weight of the spear and then threw it as hard as I could at the target. It hit the target, but in the upper right corner.

Hephaistos shook his head and then smiled sadistically. "I know two weapons she'll love." He snapped his fingers and a long, curved sword and two identical axes appeared on the ground in front of me. I'd never handled a knife before, so I wasn't sure why he thought I'd like these weapons, but I picked the sword up anyways, twirling it around to get used to the feel and weight of it.

Ares stepped in front of me with a sword in his hand. "You attack and I'll defend myself."

I nodded and ran a hand along the side of the shiny blade. Something felt familiar about it. I turned to Ares and taking a two handed grip, began attacking. Ares blocked every single swing I took, but he was smiling, so I must have been doing something right.

Ares pointed to the axes. "Try those."

I set the sword down carefully and then picked up the two axes. I was worried about handling two items at once, but after flipping them around a few times, they felt like extensions of my hands.

I turned back to Ares and found him with a shield and a thick spear. He hit the spear against the shield. "Attack."

Some primal part of me took over, my blood pumping harder and my attention focused on Ares. I charged forward, a battle cry slipping from my mouth as I swung the axes, meeting his shield and spear again and again. Frustration built in me. I wanted blood.

Doubling my effort, I surged forward and spun the axes together as I ran toward Ares. He brought his shield up, but the axes cut through the shield, cleaving it in half and then made a small cut on Ares' arm. I watched as golden blood dripped from his cut, down his arm, and to the ground. The instant it touched the grass the pounding of my heart and the adrenaline drained away, making me feel sick. I dropped the axes and sank to the ground on my knees.

I looked up to find Ares' eyes black as onyx and filled with anger. He looked at me and I groveled at his feet. "I'm sorry. Please forgive me. I don't know what overcame me."

Ares cleared his throat a few times and then whispered, "There is no need to apologize. That is exactly what I was hoping for."

I looked up and watched as his wound stopped bleeding and closed up, his skin became unmarred and perfect again. Ares waved towards the house. "Go. You're done for today. I'll be back tomorrow to train with you more."

I stood up and started to walk away, but it felt wrong to leave the sword and axes on the ground. I picked up the sword and Hephaistos handed me a leather sheath. "Here, this way you can carry them on you without worrying about cutting yourself."

I slipped the sword into the sheath and then slid the sheathed sword over my shoulder to lie across my back. I tried to draw the sword, but my long hair got in the way. Irritated, I quickly braided my hair and tossed the braid over the other shoulder so I could draw my weapon uninhibited. I picked up the axes and frowned. I'd seen men carry axes on a belt strapped around their waist, but in my knee-length tunic it would look strange.

Hephaistos noticed my problem and snapped his fingers. A strange leather harness of some sort appeared in his hands. He gently repositioned my sword so that it was vertical along my spine, with the hilt hidden beneath my hair and then placed the leather harness, which was actually just an array of straps to fit around my shoulder to hold the axes at angles across my back so that I could pull both by simply reaching both arms over the opposite shoulders and lift the axes out.

I practiced pulling and sheathing the axes a few times until I was sure the position was good and then tried to pull my sword, but my arms weren't used to the position and it was an awkward movement.

Ares said, "You'll get used to it after a while."

I bowed to Ares and then Hephaistos. "Thank you for your gifts."

Hephaistos smiled. "Oh, they're not gifts. I'm simply returning what was rightfully yours."

"Mine?"

He nodded his head. "Those are Achilles' weapons. I've been keeping them safe until I could return them."

Is that why they'd seemed familiar? Surely I didn't possess part of Achilles' mind in me. Or did I? "Thank you, Hephaistos. I'll be sure to take good care of them."

Chapter 2

Training with the sword and axes was the easiest training I'd ever done. It was like my body had come pre-programmed for their use. The day I was to fight Apollo, I awoke in a cold sweat. How could I possibly fight him now, knowing that he had been courting me? And why would any god want me as a wife when I couldn't bear children? Yes, one of the side effects to being made from a mortal's bones is that even though we were living and had all the same parts, we were infertile. Of course, it meant no monthly bleeds, which was a blessing, if you asked me.

I stood in my chambers dressed in my knee-length tunic, my sword and axes strapped on my back, and my hair in a tight braid which trailed down to the top of my rump. I, Achillia, Servant of Eros, was about to fight Apollo, the youthful god whose symbol was a silver bow and arrow. Right now I would have felt better about fighting Artemis.

"Would you really?" asked a strong female voice.

I spun around and stared in awe at Artemis, Goddess of the Hunt, standing in my chambers. "Goddess Artemis!" I started to drop to the ground, but she caught my arm and smoothed out my tunic.

"Calm now, dear. I'm not here to smite you or any such thing. I understand what you were thinking and it wasn't as an insult to me." She walked around me while she spoke, slowly looking over my body.

"Why are you here then, if you don't mind my asking?"

Artemis stopped and smiled at me. "I've come to give you some advice and to cheer you on. You see, my brother and I have been rivals with the bow and arrow since we were born and I'd very much like to see you best him."

I sighed. "I'm sorry to disappoint you, Artemis, but my sword and axes are no match for the arrows of a god."

Artemis smiled. "Oh, but they will be once I give you the secret...and my gift."

Gifts from gods were sometimes dangerous, often required payment, and not always what they first appeared to be. Pandora's gift for example.

"What gift? And what do I have to do in order to keep the gift without dying some ugly, horrible death?" I asked.

Artemis laughed. "Yes, I do like you. I can see now why Apollo was visiting you so frequently. I give you this gift as the Goddess of the Hunt to a young huntress. No strings attached, no repayment necessary. If you use it, you won't die or burst into flames or condemn yourself to never find a man. No, this is just a gift to be used to assist you in your hunting and fighting." She pulled my sword from its sheath and ran her hands down it. "I miss Achilles, he was a great warrior."

She seemed to be talking to herself, so I stayed silent. She stared at the sword a moment longer before holding it in both palms and speaking quickly and quietly in the language of the gods. The sword glowed brighter and brighter until I had to shield my eyes from fear of going blind. Artemis stopped chanting, the light disappeared, and when I opened my eyes, the sword was gone. "Wha…? I thought you were giving me a gift, not taking my sword?"

Artemis wagged her finger at me in reproach. "Nasty words won't get you anywhere."

"Sorry, Goddess Artemis."

She smiled. "Good girl. Now, take your sword."

Apparently, the rumors about her losing a few marbles had been right. Artemis rolled her eyes and thrust her hands at me. "Pick it up!"

I reached out to where the handle of the sword used to be and gasped when I gripped it. The sword was invisible!

"In order to make it become visible or invisible, you simply have to think it and it will obey."

Visible.

The sword returned visible in my hand.

Invisible.

The sword disappeared from view.

"This is amazing!" I exclaimed as I sheathed it, still invisible.

"Now, for the secret. My brother will not aim at your heart for he is fond of it, but he cannot afford to appear weak either, after Heracles challenged him. So, he will aim for your left shoulder. What you should do to protect yourself is, hold your invisible sword in your right hand, but also make your left hand into a fist, similar to the way you hold your sword. This way Apollo won't know that you are holding a sword, but he'll think you're making fists in nervousness. When you hear the twang of his bow string, flick your sword up to disrupt its path and protect yourself. I guarantee it'll take him at least four arrows before he's figured out what you're doing and by then you should have made enough ground to attack him hand to hand. If not, I cannot help you."

This secret alone could win me the battle. Why would she help me defeat him? Surely it wasn't just to see Apollo fail.

Artemis smiled. "Still wary of me?"

I smiled. "I don't mean to seem ungrateful, but the gods aren't known for being kind all the time. You often play cruel jokes on others simply for your amusement."

Artemis nodded her head. "I'm glad you are wary of even the gods. It will serve you well on your journey."

"Journey? What journey?" I asked in confusion.

Artemis waved her hand dismissively. "Everyone has a journey at some point in their lives. Just do as I've instructed and try your hardest to defeat Apollo." I expected her to disappear with a snap of her fingers, but instead she walked out of my door. Today was definitely going to be a weird day.

I walked out the door and toward the grassy area where the fight was to be held. The entire House of Eros was in attendance, which I expected, but I hadn't expected so many high ranking gods to attend as well. Ares, Eros, Athene, Hephaistos, Heracles, Artemis, and even Hades had come to witness this fight.

I swallowed my nerves and marched on to the field, bowing before the assembled group of gods. "It is an honor to be in the presence of so many great gods and goddesses. I hope I do not disappoint you."

Athene looked down her pointed nose at me and said, "Yes, let's hope you don't."

Ares rolled his eyes discreetly and motioned for me to stand. "Are you ready, Achillia?"

I nodded and stretched my arms and legs. "Yes."

"I'm ready," said Apollo from behind me. I straightened up

slowly and turned around to find him wearing full battle armor. He looked at my outfit and frowned. "Hm, it seems I'm overdressed." I watched, hormones raging, as he stripped out of his armor until he was wearing only his tunic and quiver and holding his bow. He picked up my hand and kissed the back of it gently. "A kiss in agreement for a fair fight."

I curtsied. "Thank you, gracious Apollo."

We walked away from each other until we were on opposite sides of the field. The crowd grew silent as Ares stood up. "You know the rules, all is fair in war, except outside interference. Begin!"

I sprinted forward, pulling my sword out and clenching my other fist as Apollo strung his first arrow. I stopped and closed my eyes, waiting for...twang. My right hand shot up, my sword snapped the arrow in two and sent it flying over my shoulder. I opened my eyes and started running again. Three quarters of the field left to go. Apollo knocked another arrow and aimed, this time I did not stop running. The instant he released the arrow, I brought my sword up, but he'd already learned my trick and had aimed at my right arm. Pain ripped through my shoulder as the arrowhead ran through my arm and out the other side. I stopped running and Artemis gasped. Blood poured down my chiton, staining it red while anger boiled in me, tinting my vision black. I snapped the arrowhead off and pulled the shaft from my arm, forcing myself not to make a noise of pain. Two of the female servants of Eros' fainted beside him.

I tossed the shaft to the ground and looked up at Apollo who had started to walk towards me. "You yield?" he asked softly.

I glared at him. "Never."

After re-sheathing my sword and pulling my axes, I started

my run towards him. Blood. I wanted Apollo's blood on my axes and my sword. He needed to pay for harming my body. How dare he harm the great Achilles, err, Achillia!

Apollo pulled out a sword from his side and raised it just in time to block my slice. I attacked as ferociously as I could, but he blocked every hit.

That was it. He was only defending, not attacking. Why? If I had to bet my soul, I'd bet that he was trying to avoid hurting me.

I pretended to slash upwards, but stopped at the last second so when his sword came down to block it, he hit my arm and opened a small cut. I screamed in pain and dropped to the ground, dropping my left ax. Apollo dropped to one knee beside me, his sword down at his side. I smiled and slashed upwards with my ax, opening a large slice in Apollo's upper arm. His blood stained my ax and the ground, but my bloodlust was not satisfied. I stood up and prepared to attack Apollo again, but he was gone. I started to turn around to search for him, but stopped when I felt a cold metal tip press against the front of my throat.

"Yield?" Apollo asked softly, his body pressed up against the back of mine.

I swallowed but that pressed the sword harder against my throat. "Yield," I said softly.

Apollo pulled the sword back and then kissed my cheek before walking away. His kiss burned softly like a sunburn for a moment before cooling. I forced myself not to rub my cheek and instead walked to Ares and bowed before him.

Ares, Apollo, Athene, and Artemis were speaking softly together in the language of the gods so I couldn't understand. I was trying to wait patiently, but my wounds were burning and my throat was drier than any desert.

Ares paused in his talk with Athene to turn to me. "You did well. You are dismissed to attend to your wounds and clean yourself."

"Thank you," I whispered as I stood up. I tried to pick up both of my axes, but the wound in my right shoulder had worsened and now I couldn't hold it.

Apollo picked the ax up and took the second one from my left hand. "I'll hold them while we walk to the healing chambers."

I wanted to argue, but he looked very intent on speaking to me, so I conceded and started walking. Eros was gone from his seat and so were the other women of the House. When had they left? Had they given up on me? Or had they just left after the fight ended? Was Eros disgusted by my performance and now disgusted with me? I was sure the women would treat me differently now.

I hadn't realized how much blood I had lost from my wound until we started the walk to the healing chambers. Every step felt like Hephaistos was pounding a hammer against my skull. My body was beginning to feel numb, but I wasn't sure if that was a good sign or not. I stopped to lean against a pillar just inside the mansion and my body swayed.

Apollo caught me as I fainted and slapped my face gently to wake me up. "Stay awake, Achillia."

"I am awake."

He brushed sweaty strands of my hair away from my face and sighed. "I hadn't meant to hurt you. I thought you had a shield on or something and was testing my theory. I'm sorry."

"Don't apologize. You were supposed to fight me and test me. If you hadn't hurt me then Heracles would have made a fuss about Artemis being the better one to test me. Besides, I cut you."

"My wounds heal almost instantly. You are on the verge of dying."

I rolled my eyes at him. "I am not dying. I'm just anemic from the loss of blood and dehydrated."

"Let me heal you," he said softly.

I looked into his eyes and saw concern and something else, something much deeper that made his eyes sparkle. What did it mean?

"Well, you are the god of healing and medicine. So, go ahead." I expected him to lay me down and chant or something, but I did not expect him to kiss me.

It was the most amazing thing I'd ever experienced and sadly was over too quickly. I sat in stunned silence for a moment until I realized that I felt completely invigorated. "You healed me with a kiss?"

Apollo looked abashed for a moment before he whispered, "I didn't use powers to heal you. I gave you part of my essence. Now you'll be much harder to hurt because your reflexes will be better and you will heal quicker."

"Oh, Zeus!" I yelled, standing up and pacing. "Apollo, do you know how much trouble I'm going to get in with Eros?" I wailed.

Apollo grabbed my arm, but I pulled away from him, wringing my hands in worry. Eros was surely going to punish me. I'd probably be whipped in front of the entire House.

Apollo grabbed both of my arms and shoved me up against a pillar. "Achillia. Stop worrying. Eros will only be mad at me and he'll soon get over it."

A blush rushed to my cheeks as I basked in the warmth of his presence. Whenever Apollo was upset the power of the sun seeped out of him. I looked up into his face and whispered, "Why do you risk so much for me?"

Apollo's grip loosened, but his heat intensified as he leaned down to whisper in my ear, "You know why."

"Step away from my servant," Eros commanded, his words sharp with anger.

Apollo stepped back and glanced towards Eros. "I was only speaking with her."

Eros grabbed my hand and pulled me towards him. "Come, Achillia. We have matters to discuss."

Apollo's skin was glowing and soon was too bright for my mortal eyes to look at. "I'll speak with you later, Achillia."

"Good night, sir," I answered respectfully as Eros drug me by the arm towards my chambers.

"Pig headed, egotistic, self-centered youth. Why he has to be so important in our hierarchy I will never know," Eros mumbled.

Eros pushed open my door and sat down in the large leather chair in the corner. He pointed to the small couch opposite the chair. "Sit, please."

The only other time he'd had a private conference with me like this was when I'd punched one of the male servants for ogling me. Was he disappointed in me for losing to Apollo? Had he already figured out what Apollo had done?

"After conferring with the others, we've come to a decision. I'd like to offer you a new position."

"A new position? You mean that promotion you were talking about?"

Eros smiled. "Yes. You know we are having problems with the warlocks and our Messordei are dwindling."

I nodded.

"You are being given the rare opportunity to become a Messordei."

I stared at him. Me, a Messordei? No. I couldn't. Not that I didn't want to. The Messordei were great looking with wings, horns and a tail that has a sharp triangular tip. The warlocks called them *devils* and some of the humans who believed in one god thought they were Satan. To us they were revered warriors.

Eros continued, "We need you to go on a special mission for us. The warlocks are attempting to close the doorway between the human world and ours. If they succeed, we will not be able to walk on earth ever again."

"You can't walk on it as it is now," I commented.

Eros nodded. "Yes, because they have already created a barrier. This doorway will be permanent if you don't find it first and destroy it."

Me? Destroy the doorway between our worlds? Defeat warlocks and witches? No, I can't. I'm not ready for something like that. Maybe in a few years with more training I could be ready.

"Achillia, this is a great honor. Just think about it." He stood, offered a small smile, and left.

I waited five minutes heading out to the field. I did my best thinking away from the other servants and the House, and especially away from Eros. To get to my thinking spot I had to walk two hundred paces from the house, turn left past the grapevines and walk six hundred paces before coming to a large field of grasses and flowers with one single oak tree standing tall and proud in the center. Some call it the "Tree of Life" but I just like to sit and think in its shade.

I plopped down at the base of the tree and inhaled the familiar smells. Instantly, I relaxed and my mind worked on my problem. My aching muscles from the fight settled and relaxed. If I became a Messordei, I would be worshipped. I would have great glory as a warrior. But, if I became a Messordei and was sent on this mission to stop the warlocks, what ending was there except death for me and failure to help the gods?

Ares couldn't possibly think this was a task I was ready for. I knew I wasn't ready. No, I was not ready to die. Not yet. Not while I still hadn't…well…done anything. Living in the House of Eros was boring except for the times I spent training with Ares, and now those training sessions would stop. I was doomed to boredom and a worthless life if I stayed in the House.

Boredom or death? Sadly, it was an easy decision.

"Death is not an absolute," said a male voice from behind me.

The voice was somewhat familiar, but I couldn't put a face to the speaker.

"Death is an absolute for mortals," I responded, but didn't feel like getting up to see who it was. My sore muscles were just too relaxed and I didn't care enough.

"Yes, but death is not absolute for you on this journey."

"What journey?" Whoever he was, he obviously knew a lot about me, which meant I should know him.

"The journey you are about to embark on."

"If you're talking about the task Eros asked me to do, I'm not going. There's no way I could complete it. I would just die a failure to him and the rest of the gods."

"If you sit here on your bum and don't even try then you've already failed."

I stood up and spun around to face the speaker. "Heracles?"

He smiled. "Hello, Achillia."

"What are you doing here?"

"I came to talk with you."

"Well, I'm not ready to do what Eros wants me to do. You

of all people should see that. If I had a few years to train, then maybe I'd be ready, but I couldn't beat—"

Heracles grabbed me by the arms and slammed me up against the tree. "You talk a lot for someone who doesn't have much to say."

"Let me go," I growled.

Heracles smiled. "Why don't you make me?"

"Right, like I'm going to win against you, a god."

"Alright, then just give up and die."

He wrapped his hands around my throat and squeezed, instantly cutting off the air from my lungs. I slapped at him and struggled, but he held firm.

In a matter of seconds, I'd black out and then he'd kill me. I had only walked a thousand paces from the House and already I was being killed.

What was I doing? I had my sword on my back and I wasn't helpless. I reached back and grabbed my still invisible sword and slashed down at Heracles, but he dropped his hold and jumped back before I could cut him. My throat burned as I gasped for air.

"So why don't you really want to go on this journey?" he asked calmly, as if he hadn't just tried to kill me.

"I don't want to die."

He smiled. "Well, you're far from helpless. You just defended yourself against an immortal. You think it'll be harder to defend yourself against average mortals?"

He had a point. "Look, I wasn't made for this. I was made to smile, bat my eyelashes and make men drool over me," I said as I dropped to the ground to sit.

Heracles shook his head. "No, that's what Eros trained you for. You were made to be beautiful, seductive, and deadly. You think Achilles batted his eyes at his enemies and they just dropped dead?"

That would make for an interesting fight. I huffed.

"And do you honestly think that Eros and Ares would send you out if they believed you were just going to die?" Heracles asked.

He was making a lot of sense, but still… "If you'll excuse me, Heracles, I must return to the House. I need to bathe after the fight I had earlier."

Heracles bowed. "Of course. I'm always around if you'd like to talk. Just think my name and summon me."

He disappeared in a flash, leaving me alone with the tree again. What was I going to do? I walked back to the House, pondering over the things Heracles had said. Maybe it wasn't hopeless. Maybe I could complete the task. I stepped into my chambers and found Eros sitting in the chair again.

Eros stood and looked me over. "Achillia, where have you been?"

"In the field with the Tree."

He sat back down and motioned for me to do the same. I sat and decided I would tell him I would accept. Eros cleared his throat. "I realized after I left that I hadn't told you what you would gain from completing this task for us. I know people won't simply complete tasks for glory anymore…"

"But, Eros—"

Eros glared at me. "…and you require more than our thanks so—"

"Eros, I don't—"

"Achillia, stop interrupting me!" Eros bellowed.

It was the first time he'd ever yelled at me.

"I know I taught you better than to interrupt a god while he is speaking."

"I apologize and beg your forgiveness," I said softly.

Eros smiled. "You are forgiven. Now, as I was saying. If you complete this task for us, not only will you be an immortal Messordei, but I will also grant you the option to choose whichever suitor you want, as long as he wants you as well, freedom so that you are no longer my servant, the ability to live wherever you choose even if it's not in this House, and one more boon of your choosing."

Zeus had to be playing a trick with me. Eros could not have possibly just offered me everything that I had ever wanted.

I stared at him. "Immortality? The kind where I wouldn't ever die?"

Eros laughed. "Yes, that kind of immortality. You didn't know the Messordei were immortal?"

I shook my head and then asked, "And I could leave here if I desired?"

"You could travel throughout the realms if you wanted."

"I'll be an immortal Messordei, able to choose my suitor, leave this House if I choose, and an additional wish of my choosing?"

"Yes."

Well that made my mind up for me. I'd never be given such a deal ever again. I doubted any mortal would receive such a deal. "I accept."

Eros smiled and extended his hand towards me. "Let's seal the deal then."

I clasped hands with him and felt power filling me. I closed my eyes and gritted my teeth as I felt my body changing. Tomorrow was definitely going to be fun.

Chapter 3

Everyone had gathered to see my new form and to see me off on my journey. My bag was already packed and sat on the ground a few feet away from me as I explored my new body. I wasn't any taller or bulkier or thinner, but I had horns on top of my head, wings which could be retracted and a tail with a triangular pointed end that seemed to move on its own. And for some reason, my chest had enlarged. I was sure that wasn't part of the normal Messordei metamorphosis, but I wasn't complaining and I didn't want to ask Eros.

Ares watched me as I somersaulted, did back flips and handstands, and jumped as high as I could. I was quicker, more agile, and could jump higher.

Ares cleared his throat. "I'd like a quick test, Achillia."

I nodded, having expected this from him. His broad sword appeared in his hand as he stepped towards me. I pulled my sword, which was currently visible, from its sheath on my back and assumed a ready stance. Ares exhaled and charged forward. I leapt up and over his head, slashing downwards, but he leaned back and put his sword up to block mine. I spun around and jogged backwards to give myself space from him, but it didn't matter because he was a god and incredibly fast. I brought my sword up just in time to block a slash at my throat. Before I could think, my tail whipped around and opened a gash on his right arm.

Ares bellowed and stepped back from me. "Damn those things hurt," he grumbled angrily.

"Sorry. I didn't mean to. It seems to have a mind of its own," I said as my tail swished back and forth in quick jerking motions behind me.

Ares smiled. "Don't apologize, and you'll soon be used to your body."

I turned around and ended up nose to nose with Apollo, well, his nose to my forehead and mine to his chest anyways. I stepped backwards and bowed. "My apologies, I didn't realize you were so close."

Apollo smiled. "You're forgiven." He walked around me slowly, looking at my body and smiling. "I like you as a Messordei. It brings out your true nature."

"Thank you." I think.

Heracles blinked into existence beside Apollo. "Hello, Achillia. I'm glad to see you survived the process."

"I didn't know there was a chance I wouldn't survive." I frowned, my tail swishing faster.

Heracles shrugged. "It was a small chance, and you didn't ask. Are you ready for your journey?"

I sheathed my sword and picked up my bag. "Yes."

Hades appeared out of a cloud of black smoke beside me. "She's not ready yet. She has one more attribute needing to be added before she leaves."

I looked from Heracles to Apollo and then back to Hades. "Okay, what is it?"

Hades smiled. "As you know Messordei are immortal, but in order for them to keep their appearance at a certain age, they must give me a gift. A soul."

"Keeping my body looking the same age is a gift from you? A soul? What?" I was really confused now.

Hades smirked. "Stand still, Achillia." He placed his hand over my mouth and then against my sternum. He whispered words I couldn't understand and then a blinding pain made me scream. Hades removed his hands and smiled. "Now, if you want to age a couple years then just restrain from feeding, but if you want to stay looking the same age then you need to absorb at least one soul every two days."

"Soul! I'm supposed to absorb a soul?" My eyes widened.

Hades smiled. "I am the God of the Underworld. So, after you kill someone you will see their soul hovering over their body, and you can just suck it into your body. I'll be able to harvest the souls from you, but don't ask how. You can also take someone's soul from them while they're alive, which is much easier to do than after they're already dead because once dead their soul will start to move on. To take someone's soul while they're alive you just lock eyes with them and you will see their soul within them. Inhale and the soul will be pulled from the host's body into yours. If you didn't eat soon enough, you will age five years and then another year for each additional ten minutes beyond an hour. You'll need to eat soon after you arrive." Hades kissed my cheek and then disappeared in his black smoke.

Despite everything he did, he was one hot-looking god. I swallowed nervously as I thought about having to kill people. I knew I had to kill warlocks, but what if there wasn't a warlock around and I needed a soul? I did not want to age faster than I was supposed to.

Heracles handed me a small purse and said, "Don't open that until you get to the mortal realm. The note inside will explain all."

I put the purse in my bag and smiled. "Thank you."

Heracles winked at me. "Be talking to you soon."

I opened my mouth to ask what he meant, but he disappeared before I could.

Apollo grabbed my hand and turned it palm up. "I have a gift for you too."

He set a golden necklace with a pendent in my hand. I picked the pendant up and frowned at the sun etched into it. "No offense, but I don't worship you."

Apollo sighed. "Things would be so much easier if you had."

I rolled my eyes at him

He sighed. "Turn it over."

I did as he said, and found a wolf etched into the back of it. One of Apollo's symbols was the wolf and I knew that an order of people in the mortal realm wore this pendant and worshipped Apollo.

"Wear this and you will find help when you arrive."

"Your worshippers will assist me?" I asked.

Apollo closed my hand around the pendant and then kissed the back of it. "I've already contacted the leader and he is expecting you."

I curtsied to Apollo and thanked him.

Ares rested his hand on my shoulder. "It's time to go."

I nodded and walked to Eros, who sat in a chair on the grass being fanned by servants. I knelt on one knee and bowed my head. "I leave now to go complete the task you have assigned to me. I will complete this task or die trying."

"Go with my blessing. And try not to die."

I looked up and saw his sadness and worry. It meant a lot to me that both he and Apollo would worry for me so much while I was away. I nodded and jogged to Ares who was already preparing to send me through. The gods could send items and people to the mortal realm and back, but they couldn't go themselves because of the barrier. Ares placed his hands on either side of my face and stared into my eyes. "Stay strong. Remember who you are and who believes in you. We'll all be watching for you, so remember to check behind your back." He kissed my forehead and whispered, "Go with my blessing and do not forget to worship the gods."

Pain exploded within my body, and I was floating in a sea of blackness. I tried to breathe, but couldn't even move my fingertips. My active tail was even lying still in the darkness.

"Who asks for permission to traverse the worlds?" asked a loud voice.

"Achillia, Messordei of Eros," I answered as I exhaled what breath I had.

"Go with our blessings and beware of the wolf for they are not always what they seem," answered the voice.

The pain disappeared and I landed on my back on stones. Groaning, I rolled over and took deep gulping breaths of air.

The human world was not what I expected. There were no luscious fields or tall trees, just a strange stone ground and tall buildings. It was night time and there were lamps lining an elevated section of stone ground where some people walked. I quickly put my hood on to hide my new horns and started my way down the street.

I took two steps, when I felt the presence of warlocks. The

presence of the warlocks was like a finger poking me in the side and a slight pressure in my head. I turned and surveyed the area around me and spotted them, two men with grey cloaks and frightening glares, which were directed at me. I was supposed to fight them, but there were humans around and I couldn't risk getting caught by them. Apollo had warned me about the dangers of something the human's called "scientists." I needed to find a deserted area to fight the warlocks.

Spinning on my heel, I marched down the walkway and turned right around the next building. In one block the area had gone from lightly traveled to completely deserted. Houses lined the streets, but all of the lights were off and the blinds were pulled. The area was wide open and rather large, with only a well in the center and a statue of a young woman pouring water from a bucket into the wall beside it. I took out my sword and prepared for my first battle.

The two warlocks rounded the corner and smiled sinisterly. Not a good sign for me.

I smiled back and prepared a shield of my new magic to deflect any of their long-range attacks. My shield looked like a red ball of flickering light and as I looked at the warlocks I felt my eagerness for a fight.

The warlocks didn't try any long-range attacks, instead they choose to charge forward, pull swords, and start attacking me. I blocked and attacked, but with two on me at once, I was put mainly on defense and I couldn't maintain my shield. I needed to find a way to attack or my stamina would run out.

One warlock spun around, and I was forced to pull one of my axes out to block the attacks from behind and use my sword to block the ones from the front. My tail swished angrily behind me and I got an idea. I smiled happily and while blocking their attacks, whipped my tail back and down, opening a large cut in the warlock behind me's leg. He yelped and slashed at my tail. I yanked it back against my leg just in time to miss his sword.

"You tried to cut off my tail!" I yelled. "I just got it!"

The warlocks looked at me with furrowed brows, and I took the opportunity to disarm them. Their swords flew in an arc and then landed in the well. The splash which sounded afterwards was like a cherry on top of a cake.

I only had a moment of victory though because at that moment my stomach decided to growl and my limbs grew heavy.

Hades had told me that I'd need to eat, but he hadn't said I'd need to eat as soon as I arrived here. If I didn't find food quickly, I would age. Once I ate though, I'd be stuck at whatever age I'd increased to and unable to go backwards. I did not want to look like much older!

I struck at the warlock in front of me, but the one behind me grabbed me around the shoulders and held on tight. I screamed in frustration, but they disarmed me and I was trapped.

"You stupid Messordei think you're so tough," spat the warlock in front of me. He walked around me and snarled. "You are nothing but an abomination and it is our job to ensure your annihilation. We will not rest until every single one of your kind is dead."

Every cell in my body vibrated with anger. Anger at being held against my will. Anger at having lost so quickly. Anger at these idiots having defeated me. "Release me!" I ordered.

The warlock holding me tightened his grip until it was painful to inhale. "We'll let go of you soon enough."

The warlock in front of me smiled and then punched me

in the face. Pain exploded along my cheek. He punched me in the stomach and what little air I had had whooshed out. I tried to gasp for breath, but the other warlock kept his hold on me. He hit me again and again, until I went limp.

Finally, they dropped me on the ground. The cool stone felt good against my swollen and bloody face. I started to get up, but then they began kicking me. I thought I was done for, but then a man said, "I think it's highly unfair for two men to beat on one woman."

The warlocks stopped their assault and turned to face the newcomer. "This isn't any of your business, stranger. Be on your way."

The newcomer said, "Two men beating up and obviously trying to kill a woman isn't any of my business? Sirs, I believe it is every man's business to protect a woman being brutally attacked."

"She's not a woman, you ignorant boy. She's a Messordei and deserves no kindness."

"Watch who you call boy!" snarled the newcomer. He started to walk forward, and the warlocks took ready stances. I tried to watch the fight, but the hunger and pain were too much. I clenched my eyes and teeth closed and hoped the warlocks wouldn't hurt the man too badly for interfering and trying to protect me.

The sounds of their fighting were strange. I heard snarls and growling, thunder, and crashing, wood splintering, and stones cracking.

The sounds stopped and hands touched me. I opened my eyes and struck out while trying to back away.

"It's alright. I won't harm you," said the newcomer.

I looked up and logical thoughts stopped. This man was handsome, possibly as handsome as Apollo, and as muscular as Ares. He was squatted before me with only a few cuts and bloody hands as the only signs that he'd been in a fight.

What he said finally sunk in and I looked to find the bodies of the two warlocks leaning against the side of the well.

I looked back at the man. "You? You killed both of them?"

He smiled. "Don't look so shocked, but no, I only knocked them out."

My stomach growled again and I doubled over. The man sat me back up. "Please, sir. I know this is going to sound awful, but I need...I need you to bring me one of them."

The man picked me up in his arms and stood up. "It doesn't sound strange at all. Darling, I'm not exactly human either."

Before I could ask what he meant, he moved me to the side of the warlock who had assaulted me the most. I stared into the warlock's eyes and saw an orb of silver. The orb of silver which I assumed was his soul swayed within him. I inhaled as hard as I could and its essence filled me.

My body began glowing red, my horns grew an inch longer, and I felt revitalized.

The man watched with curiosity, but no fear. What was he if not human and not fearful of me?

My wounds were still unhealed, but I didn't want to kill the other warlock. I had dreaded taking the life and soul of a person once Hades had informed me that was how Messordei survived and I didn't want to take the life of someone to heal wounds which would heal on their own.

The man picked me back up and then retrieved my sword and ax from the ground where the warlocks had thrown them. "You may rest, young woman. I will protect you and take you to my home where you will be safe while you recuperate."

"You don't even know me. Why would you do this for me?" I asked in shock

He touched the necklace Apollo had given me. "I am a worshipper of Apollo. I help any of his chosen. Especially, the one he entrusted me to protect."

He was the one Apollo had told me about. My eyes widened as I studied his face.

The man smiled at my expression, and then started running again. He was definitely not human, because he moved too fast. I started to doze off when he stopped running and opened a door. I opened my eyes and stared at the wooden two-story house we were walking into. He carried me up the stairs and into a room which was easily twice the size of mine at Eros' house.

The man set me down on the large fluffy bed and then disappeared through a side door. I relaxed on the bed and closed my eyes. I would have to find some gift for Apollo for giving me this man to protect me. I would have died if not for him.

I started to fall asleep and then felt a damp cloth against my face. "I'm sorry I wasn't there sooner," said the man.

"What's your name?" I asked softly.

He continued to clean my face gently and said, "I'm Max. What's your name?"

"Achillia," I whispered as he wiped at an area with dried blood.

"What are you?" he asked.

I opened my eyes and found him staring at me intently. I swallowed nervously. "I used to be a servant of Eros, but then

I was picked for a mission and granted the privilege of becoming a Messordei. I was just changed and sent here."

He blinked at me and then asked, "You're a Messordei?"

I nodded my head sadly. "Not a very good one as you could tell."

He shrugged and resumed cleaning my face. "You're young and new to your powers. In time you'll grow into them."

"I don't want to grow into them. I don't have time to. I have to complete this mission quickly."

"You aren't going to be doing anything today except eating and resting. Tomorrow is a new day, and I will help you in your quest."

"What are you, Max?" I was trying not to be rude, but curiosity got the better of me. Pandora wasn't the only female who was overly curious.

Max set the cloth down and moved a little away from me to give me space. "You know of Lycaon?"

I nodded my head. "The mortal who tried to feed Zeus human flesh and was turned into a wolf."

Max nodded his head. "I am a descendent of Lycaon."

I shook my head. "You can't be. He died in the flood."

Max smiled. "Lycaon may have been disrespectful, but he was no fool. He found a hiding place which did not flood all the way to the top and brought in fish for him to eat. He survived the flood."

This was something no one had ever told me. Did the gods know? Surely Zeus was aware that Lycaon was alive. "If you are a descendent then why aren't you a wolf?" I asked.

Max smiled wider. "I am." He stepped off the bed and I watched in disbelief as red light surrounded his body and then the man changed into a wolf. He changed back again and said, "I'm part wolf. The humans refer to us as 'lycanthropes' or 'werewolves'."

In all my life I'd never expected to find a mystical being not in Olympus on Earth. I'd met centaurs, minotaurs, nymphs, and even a Pegasus, but never a man who could become a wolf. How had Apollo gained their worship? One of his symbols was a wolf, but was that the only reason they chose him as their patron god?

"What are you thinking?" he asked me softly.

"That I never expected to find a man-animal on earth that I hadn't met in Olympus."

Max's eyes widened. "Olympus? You've been there?"

I frowned. "I told you I was a servant of Eros, the God of Love. I worked in his house and frequently visited with other gods."

Max stared at me.

I blushed. "Not that type of visiting. Just friendly visiting and visits from Ares for battle."

"You know Ares?" he asked, taking a step closer to me.

"Yes. I trained with Ares, sparred with Heracles, and fought against Apollo."

I didn't think Max' eyes could get any wider, but they did. "You...fought against...Apollo?"

I smiled. "Yes. He's one of my friends."

Max sat in the chair by the door. "I'd give anything to meet Apollo face to face. He visits my dreams, but to actually meet the God of the Sun in person would be amazing. Or to meet Ares. That would be a blessing."

"Well if you want to meet them you're going to have to help me stop the warlocks. I need to find the door so the gods will be allowed to travel between worlds again."

"I've sworn to assist you in any way I can."

I looked at him and couldn't help the smile that formed on my lips. I quickly hid it by turning away from him. "Thank you. For today. I would have died if not for your assistance."

Max touched my arm softly and turned me around. "You need not thank me. Rest now, and I'll come get you when it's time for supper."

He shut the door softly behind him, and I climbed up into the bed. Hopefully my face wouldn't look so frightening tomorrow morning. I closed my eyes and fell asleep. At least my body was sleeping. I was standing inside a house, much like Eros'.

"I see you've made it to the human world," said an all-too-familiar voice.

"Heracles," I said softly.

He smiled at me from his throne in the back of the room. "Achillia. You look like you've had a fun time already."

I rolled my eyes at him. "Yeah, two warlocks were there when I arrived. Not a great way to start my trip."

Heracles walked to me and examined my face. "You should learn to block the punches with something other than your face."

I rolled my eyes at him again. "While I find your insights extremely helpful, do you have something to say or can I go to sleep?"

"I've received word from one of my Messordei. They've found a large contingent of warlocks guarding an area near the town of Twin Falls. We believe this is the location of the door. You are to meet them in two days with any assistance you can find." I thought of Max and Heracles frowned. "Who are you thinking of?"

I blushed. "Just a helper that Apollo gave me."

"Focus on the task at hand, Achillia. You can indulge in your impulses once the task has been completed."

My jaw dropped, and then anger covered my shock. "Heracles, I insist you apologize at once. I have done nothing to warrant such a statement."

Heracles sighed. "I apologize. I'm just worried for you. It angers me to see you injured."

"If it weren't for Apollo's helper then I would have been killed," I said through clenched teeth. I tried to let go of my anger, but it was harder to do than normal.

Heracles turned to face out one of his windows. "Then I shall have to thank him if he continues to keep you alive."

"Heracles, I'm sorry. It's hard to control my anger right now."

Heracles turned back around and smiled. "It's alright. I understand that it's often difficult to control your anger when you first become Messordei. Meet up with the other Messordeis in Twin Falls with your helper and assess the situation. Do not engage until you are sure you can win. Good luck, Achillia and may all of the gods be with you."

The dream dissipated, and I woke up feeling fully rested instead of tired as I had expected.

"Who visited you?" asked Max from the chair by the door.

I turned to face him slowly. His face was completely blank, no emotion visible, which meant he was trying his hardest to hide what he was thinking. "Do you know where Twin Falls is?" I asked.

Max lifted a brow, but simply nodded. "It's a day's journey from here."

"Can you take me there tomorrow?"

Max nodded. "Yes. We will leave at dawn. Are you hungry for human food?"

I nodded and rubbed my stomach. "Souls only feed part of my hunger and keep me from aging..." I gasped and jumped up in search of a mirror. My bruises and the swelling were gone, my horns were long, sticking up out of my hair, but none of that registered to me. I ground my teeth together in frustration. I'd aged at least two years. I couldn't let myself age anymore.

"Is there something wrong?" Max asked from behind me.

I spun around and pointed at my face. "This! Do you see this?"

He looked carefully at each part of my face. "Yes. I see nothing wrong with it. It's quite beautiful, if you ask me."

I blushed and turned around to face the mirror again. "I've aged at least two years. Two years! Hades should have told me how soon I'd need to eat. I refuse to get any older."

"You look more like a woman now," Max said softly.

I spun around and stared at him in shock. "What?"

He smiled and my heart began beating harder. "You were youthful looking when I first saw you, but now you look like a woman, a young woman, but very beautiful." He took a step towards me and touched one of my horns. "I never thought I'd say this to a woman, but, horns are sexy."

I blushed and grabbed a hold of my tail which had been swishing behind me. "Thank you."

He stepped back from me and headed out of the room. I slowed my breathing and then followed him. Heracles was right, I needed to pay attention to the task at hand. I couldn't be one of the Messordei who lost their way on a journey because of their hormones.

Max was waiting at the bottom of the stairs for me and waved his hand. "Come, I'm hungry."

I hurried to catch up to him as he led me to a dining room

which had a table long enough to fit ten people and was filled to that limit except for two chairs on the ends. Max walked to the head of the table and motioned for me to take the other chair. All of the people sitting at the table were men and watched me with wary eyes. I could feel the similarity of their auras and also the difference of them from humans. More Lycaon descendants.

"Please sit, Achillia."

I sat in the chair, and all heads swiveled away from me to Max. Max nodded to them. "Achillia is the one Apollo contacted me about. She will be staying with us while she completes her task for the gods, and I expect you all to protect her as though she were one of our female pups."

The men at the table nodded and then went silent. A woman in her mid-twenties walked into the room with a pitcher of ice water. She stopped when she saw me and growled. The growl surprised me due to its animal quality even though she was in human form. She started to move towards me, but one of the men sitting at the table stood in her path. He looked to be about eighteen and had blonde hair and baby blue eyes. The woman cowered away from him and backed towards the kitchen. "Apologize to our guest," he said angrily.

The woman kept her eyes on the ground and said, "I apologize, Max, for dishonoring you."

The man who had stopped her earlier, started to move towards her, but Max blocked him and rested a hand on his shoulder. "I will deal with you later," Max said.

The woman nodded, glanced up to glare at me, and then scurried away. Max placed a hand on the man who was standing's shoulder and whispered, "Derek, you can deal with her insubordination later. For now, let us eat."

Derek exhaled and nodded his head. "Yes, Alpha."

Why do they keep calling Max "Alpha"?

Two other women came in and served everyone food. They glared at me with open hostility, but made no move to harm me. Why were they upset with me? I hadn't done anything to them. The food they set before me looked delicious, and I dug in greedily. I knew I still needed to eat human food, but I didn't think I'd need to eat as much as I did. Three servings later I was finally full and leaned back in my chair to look at the men around the table. All of the men were in great physical shape, warrior-like, but beyond that they were all completely different.

The rest of the meal went without incident, but that was probably because no more women came in. It felt wrong to be sitting at the table and not serving anyone, but I stayed in my seat while the group discussed issues I didn't understand.

Derek and Max started whispering to each other and one of the men next to me asked, "So, what does Apollo really look like?"

Talking ceased, and all eyes turned to me. "Um, well, he is handsome like most of the other gods, but he is a more youthful handsome. When he gets angry he starts glowing and you feel like you're standing on the sun's surface. When he is happy it feels like the sun warming your face on a clear spring day. He acts quiet and reserved, but when he's angry he is as deadly as Ares or Artemis. He has golden hair which looks like it was spun from the rays of the sun and the most..."

I stopped talking when I realized what I was saying and a blush covered my cheeks.

"It sounds like you're quite intimate with the gods," said Max with a blank face.

I sighed. "I was a servant of Eros." The men all looked at each other and shrugged. "The god of love?"

"Oh," said all of the men.

"You were his servant?" Max asked in a tight voice.

I nodded. "I helped the other servants keep up the House by performing my designated chores, which were mainly gardening. Until Ares came and started working with us on fighting to choose one of us as a Messordei."

"Ares trained you?" Derek asked, eyes wide.

I nodded. "He told me after training with me for a while that he had created me from Achilles' bones in the hopes that I would become a Messordei." I left out the part about him wanting me to be Eros' wife too.

"How many gods do you know?" asked Derek.

"I've met all of them, but I am friends with Apollo, Heracles, Ares, and Zeus."

"That's amazing," whispered one of the men.

"Could you imagine meeting the gods?" said another.

"Were any of them your suitors?" asked Max.

I blushed. "I did not have any declared suitors, but Ares told me one who apparently favored me." I shook my head. "But none of that matters. If I don't accomplish my task then I won't be able to return."

"We will leave first thing in the morning to meet with the other Messordei," said Max. He looked at his pack, "I'll be away for two days, but you should be able to deal without me for that long."

The men nodded in understanding. "Can I come?" asked Derek.

Several of the men smiled and then looked down at the table to hide their faces.

Max frowned in thought for a moment, but shook his head. "No, you need to stay here and keep the pack in order."

Derek sighed. "Fine."

I stood and started to pick up the plates, but Derek grabbed my hand when I reached for his. "You are a guest. You do not need to clean up after us."

His skin was hot, and I could taste the excitement pouring out of his skin. "I'm sorry. It's a habit."

He smiled and I pulled my hand back, setting the plates that I had collected down on top of his before walking out the front door and into the cool air. I wrapped my arms around myself and took deep cleansing breaths. I'd never experienced predators like them before. It was frightening and, if I was being honest with myself, a little exciting. The door opened and closed and Max stepped up next to me. "I'm sorry if he frightened you. He's a good boy, but he doesn't know how to behave around beautiful women who are not werewolves."

"Well then, he should have no problem dealing with me, since I'm not beautiful," I said as I sat down on the edge of the porch.

"Are you upset about what happened with the women?" he asked as he leaned against a post.

I shook my head. "No, they're just protective and don't like an unknown female encroaching on their territory." I looked up at him. "How many of them are you sleeping with? If you don't mind my asking."

He blinked slowly with a confused look on his face. "I'm not sleeping with any of them."

I shrugged. "Alright, you don't have to tell me. I was just curious."

"I'm telling you. I haven't slept with any of them."

I looked up at his serious face. "No woman looks at a man

like they look at you unless the man is sleeping with her or she's trained to look at men like that."

"They look at me adoringly because I'm their Alpha. I am the one they depend on for protection and comfort," he said.

"Oh." Well that was different. But if he had all these women why not sleep with them? Most males would.

"Werewolves mate for life," he said quietly. "That's why I don't sleep with them."

I sucked in a breath and blinked at him.

He smiled. "No, I can't read your mind. That's just what anyone would be thinking.

I blushed and looked down at my legs. Why did this man embarrass me so much? Even the gods didn't make me this nervous.

"Alpha," said a woman in front of us. "Who is your pet?"

"You will treat our guest with respect, Betina. Achillia is the one I have been chosen to protect for Apollo," said Max with a growl in his voice.

The old woman squatted down in front of me and inhaled loudly. "You're not right, are you dear?"

"What do you mean?" I asked angrily. Why did people always think something was wrong with me?

"You aren't built as a woman should be. I can smell the difference in you, or the lack of smell I should say," she said as her nostrils flared again.

I smiled. "Oh, you mean because I don't menstruate? No, I was not created for the purpose of bearing children."

"You can't have children?" Max eyed me with surprise.

I looked up at him and shook my head. "No. All of Eros' servants are created for pleasure and to avoid the unfortunate side-effect, we are built without ovaries."

"You have the other, parts, though?" she asked softly.

I nodded. "No one would know by looking at me or, um, using me, but I do not menstruate and cannot get pregnant."

"Interesting," she said as she stood and walked away. "It was nice meeting you, Achillia."

I watched as the woman walked away and wondered if she really had been curious or if she had an ulterior motive.

"We should get some sleep since we're leaving at dawn," said Max.

I nodded and followed him back into the house. "So, where will I be sleeping?" I asked softly.

He smiled. "In my bed." My heart fluttered, and he said, "Don't worry; I'll be in wolf form on the end. I'm not trying to seduce you."

I laughed. "Good, because Eros forbade anyone from using me. I'd hate to have you killed by a lightning bolt because of a misunderstanding on your part."

Max didn't see the humor in what I said and instead walked to Derek who was watching us intently. "Derek, you are in charge, effective now. At dawn Achillia and I will leave and won't return for at least three days. Don't come searching for us unless we've been gone five days with no contact."

Derek looked nervous about this, but said, "Yes, Max."

Chapter 4

Dawn came too early for me and it was strangely saddening not to hear Apollo's shouts. Max had behaved himself like he promised and slept at my feet in his wolf form. It was amazing how safe he made me feel. We set off on our journey and after a few minutes of me trying and failing to keep up with him, Max picked me up and ran. "How long can you maintain this speed?" I asked as I turned my face against his chest to avoid the press of wind against me.

"About four hours at this pace, but I can do slightly slower for about ten hours. Endurance is necessary when the beings pursuing you have claws and sharp canines."

I laughed and said, "If I get too heavy for you, I don't mind walking."

"You weigh no more to me than an infant to a mother."

Now he was just teasing me. "Well the offer still stands."

I felt like a ten-year-old girl again, when Eros had to carry me after a fall from a pegasus. I closed my eyes and dreamed of Olympus and the demigod games I so loved to watch.

"Achillia," Max whispered. "We're here."

A tingling sensation covered my body and made me grind my teeth due to how uncomfortable I felt. Max set me down on my feet and I whispered, "There're at least ten warlocks."

"You can sense them?"

I nodded.

"Ten shouldn't be too difficult to handle," he said calmly as he surveyed the area. Ahead was a single building. It was large and there were two guards standing beside the only door that led in.

Something didn't seem right. Where was the other Messordei I was supposed to meet?

We continued to survey the area, but there was no sign of the Messordei and no change.

A man screamed from inside their base.

I started to move, but Max grabbed my arm. "Wait. We can't just rush in."

Another scream echoed around us.

Max shifted into a half-wolf, half-man form. "Okay," he said and nodded.

I drew my weapons and ran as fast as I could to the entry-way. The two guards were dead before they could even open their mouths.

The door was locked, but Max ripped it off its hinges and tossed it aside. He bowed and waved me in. "Ladies first."

I smiled and ran inside. A long hallway, with five doors branching off, met us. One door was closed. Taking the chance, I headed to that door.

The Messordei screamed on the other side. I waved at Max. "Brawns before beauty."

His smile was slightly terrifying in his current form. With

one kick, the door crumpled and we shot inside the room, sliding across the floor.

Eight males looked up from where they were torturing a young male Messordei, strapped to a metal table.

Max and I growled and swept into action. It was like we had been fighting together for years. We flowed around each other, attacking and protecting the other's back with no verbal communication.

With just two warlocks left, I turned to help the Messordei, trusting Max to handle them.

"It's too late for me," he said. His face looked like he was in his sixties. "They don't know where the door is. They're looking for it, too. If you find it before them—"

"Okay, stop talking," I ordered him.

He smiled and closed his eyes. "I'm looking forward to returning to Olympus."

I set my hand on his until the last bit of life left him.

Max held two of the warlocks up by their throats. Their faces were turning purple, but they were alive. "Hungry?" he asked.

"Starving," I snarled and grabbed the warlocks, consuming their souls. I didn't bother with the already dead ones. I didn't need more, but I wanted to kill them all.

Max shifted and picked me up. "Let's go home."

Home? I didn't have a home.

Purpose. I definitely had that. I would find the door and release the gods. And, I would destroy as many warlocks and witches as I could along the way.

Chapter 5

TWO HUNDRED YEARS LATER

Chapter 6

I sat on the concrete bench leaning against the cool brick wall watching the humans before me. The first day of school was starting out cool, but I knew the heat would appear before half-day. I didn't need to be here at the high school attending classes, but the alternatives were boring. I had already matriculated once and I only attended now to avoid working, being bored at home, or aging anymore. My body and face appeared as though I were nineteen, but I could pass for a high schooler still. The body I held now served me well these past two hundred years and I didn't want to age anymore unless absolutely necessary.

I inhaled and smelled wolf fur and trees. I turned my head to the right and a boy who looked about the age of fifteen waved at me. I raised my hand in response and he bowed his head before walking away. He was older than he looked, but like me he enjoyed a youthful body and not being bored at home or finding a job.

Three girls ran up to each other hugging and squealing in delight. They began talking quickly about their summers and what important gossip the others had missed. Boys stood on the sidelines checking out which girls had matured over summer and deciding who they would try to pick up next. The first day of school was the most fun for me to human-watch. They were so focused on their little lives that they were blind to everything else. Truly amazing.

I didn't have anyone at this school to squeal at or anyone deciding when I was ready for picking up, and that's just the way I liked it. I watched the humans for a few more minutes before walking towards my first class of the day. I continually tested the air and my surroundings for any sign of my enemy, but like usual, the school was free of any threat. I walked into the classroom and sat down in a chair in the back center.

I tilted the chair back to lean against the wall balancing on its two back legs. My backpack was very light, but still held my journal and pen. The pen was cold in my hand as I opened my journal to the last page I had written on. I uncapped the pen and started writing.

D*ate: August 24, 2009*
Years on Earth: 200 years
First day of school and the humans are the same as they have been the past forty years. The women are a little more aggressive towards the men, but overall exhibit similar mentalities and actions. They are still completely ignorant to the existence of preternatural beings living among them. A truly depressing race for me to be around.

The bell rang in my ears for a moment. I put the pen and journal away as kids began filing in. Some smiled as they walked in, while some frowned. Emotions were always very mixed about this time of the year, but one emotion that ran strong was nervousness. The teacher entered, and I let my mind go blank. My first two classes passed relatively quickly as I watched the pitiful humans so unknowing of the battle going on around them. One day soon, they would meet the gods again and then the humans would be back to serving as they should. Class ended, so I walked slowly to the middle of the school where a small batch of pine trees grew. The trees were small, but vibrated with youthful energy.

I leaned against one of the pines, feeling the pressure of my sword, invisible to human eyes, sheathed on my back. My lunch consisted of only a sandwich and chips, since I ate larger meals at night and had my snack on the way home. My attitude had deteriorated from when I first arrived, but I was still focused on my goal. Not accomplishing it for so long, was rather depressing. And, I was feeling more and more like a pawn in this war between witches and warlocks and gods.

I tore off a piece of my sandwich and took one of the chips holding both of them in my right hand. "I give you this token of my servitude to you Eros, God of love and my creator. Accept this share of my meal in thanks of you providing it for me." I set the chip on the ground and watched as it absorbed in to the dirt. A cool breeze brushed across my cheek making me smile. "You're welcome."

I held a second piece of my sandwich in my hand and said, "I give you this token of my servitude to you Ares, God of war and my mentor. Accept this share of my meal in thanks of you providing it for me." I set it down and it absorbed quickly, a hot breeze blew against my arms as his sign of thanks.

I was finishing my sandwich when I sensed magic nearby. I turned my head and surveyed my surroundings, but couldn't see anyone. I finished my sandwich and picked my bag up, trying to act as normal as possible so I wouldn't draw attention to myself. I walked towards my next class scanning the areas around me, but the magic was gone. Had I imagined it? I rolled my neck and shook out my hands to release the tension. I stepped in to the classroom as the bell rang and took my normal seat in the center back row of the classroom. I tilted my chair back so that it balanced on the back two legs and leaned against the wall behind me. I liked repetitive normalcy.

I closed my eyes and focused on my right hand, making a flame spark between my finger and thumb. I opened my eyes, took the flame between both of my hands, and rolled it around until it was a small ball and began bouncing it from one hand to the other.

Other students came in and sat down far away from me, occasionally trying to sneak a glance at me from the corners of their eyes. At the moment, I looked completely human. None could tell the difference in me except when I allowed the non-human parts out. None except a select few and my enemies knew of my traits to begin with, and I liked to keep it that way. Humans were fascinated by the strange and I preferred to experiment, not be experimented on.

The creative writing class was my favorite for human-watching. I loved hearing and reading the human ideas of fantasy. There were so many things that they were correct about and yet they believed them to be fiction. Would it truly terrify them to know that vampires, werewolves, fairies, ogres, and dragons roamed the earth?

Yes. Humans liked their bubble of what was real and what wasn't, and I learned from the incident in England that you do not burst their bubble or they go crazy looking for witches and werewolves. It took me decades to make up for that fiasco.

The second bell rang, and I sensed the magic again. The fire ball extinguished in my hand as I focused on the scent of the magic nearby. It came closer and closer making me increasingly nervous. My chair dropped to all four legs on the ground, and I rested my hands flat on top of the table. It was definitely a warlock, and he was powerful. I stared at the door as it opened. My hands began glowing as a boy about the age of sixteen stepped through the door. He looked around the classroom, but seemed not to notice me. He sat two seats away, leaning his chair back against the wall as I had been. He should have noticed me and should be freaking out, like I was. What was he trying to pull? I shook my hands out so they would stop glowing and he looked over at me.

"Hi, I'm Bryce. I'm new here," he said in a perfectly pitched male voice. He extended his hand to me, and I stared at it.

Did he think I was stupid? If I touched his hand, he would more than likely try to overpower me with magic to kill me. No, I wouldn't let that happen, but I still had to play human. "I'm Achillia."

He let his hand drop to his side, and I saw the flinch, but he didn't let that stop his smile. "That's a beautiful name. What does it mean?"

I swallowed. "Daughter of Achilles."

His eyes widened. "Are you really a descendant of Achilles?"

I frowned. "That's a dumb question. Of course I am."

Bryce continued to smile at me. "Really? I'd love to hear…"

Mr. Kittle, our teacher cleared his throat interrupting Bryce. "Welcome everyone." Mr. Kittle was one of the few genuinely sweet teachers I had met. He strived to help his students. He was one of the rare humans I could stand to listen to. Unfortunately, with the warlock so close to me, my attention wasn't as focused as it usually was. I leaned my chair back taking my journal and pen out and made a note to research Bryce's family.

Class dragged on for much longer than usual as my body thrummed with anticipation of Bryce's potential attack. When the bell rang, I rushed out of the classroom and towards the parking lot. Fourth period would have to wait another day. I couldn't stay at the school with that warlock any longer. I walked quickly out to the student parking lot and towards my car. Two boys were staring at the car in awe. I hit my remote unlock making the car chirp and the boys jumped back. They stared at me, wide-eyed, as I opened the door of the 2010 Aston Martin Vantage.

One of the boys finally grew brave and asked, "Is that the V12 Vantage?"

I nodded as I pulled the vertical door down. "Yep." I started the car and backed away before they could ask me about the cars specifications. Boys were so addicted to cars in this world. Sure, I drove a very sweet car, but that was because I liked having nice things. I drove out of the parking lot and towards the house I lived in. I hadn't had a place feel like home in over two hundred years, so I didn't call it home, but just my dwelling. I pulled into the garage and walked up the stairs to the backdoor of the small Victorian cottage I owned.

I was grumbling to myself as I stepped through the door

and onto broken glass. I stopped and slowly moved my hand back just above my left shoulder, grabbing the hilt of my sword. I pulled it out of its sheath and the sword became visible. I walked slowly forward, through the kitchen and heard growling in another room. The walls were dented with body prints and blood smeared the floors.

I stepped through the kitchen door and into the living room and blinked at the two horse-sized wolves, snarling at each other. I pointed my sword at the red wolf while talking to the grey wolf, "Zack, who is your new friend and why is he bleeding on my thirteenth century Egyptian rug?"

The red wolf growled and snapped his teeth at me.

I frowned. "Don't get snippy with me! You're going to pay for my carpet to get cleaned. Do you know how hard it was to keep this thing in good shape for the hundred years I've owned it?"

The red wolf snapped his teeth once more, then darted out of the room. The grey wolf, Zack, ran after him, leaving claw marks in my rug. "Stupid werewolves are always breaking things and bleeding everywhere!" I re-sheathed my sword and started cleaning everything up.

I had a cleaning service for these types of things, but it was habit.

Zack walked in, naked and smeared with blood. "He got away. Dang it, Max is going to be pissed."

I shrugged. "Just tell your alpha that I interfered. He'll let you off."

Zack frowned, taking notice of my attitude for the first time. "Why are you upset?"

I sighed and set the broken lamp back down on the ground. "There's a warlock at school. He didn't try anything and didn't even act like anything was wrong."

Zack frowned harder. "Give me his name and I'll have Max look into him."

I shook my head. "I need to go see Max anyways. I missed my weekly visit to him. Come on, we'll explain about the red wolf getting away too."

I changed quickly into a cutoff shirt and low hip huggers that showed off my belly button ring and accentuated my perfect abs. Zack washed off the blood, and changed into a pair of blue jeans, the uniform of wereanimals. It seemed that blue jeans were the cheapest clothing that covered their lower body, while allowing for easy shredding in transformation and not causing harm to the animal changing. Zack and I climbed into his lifted Dodge truck and drove towards the werewolves' compound. I closed my eyes and leaned back against the seat playing with the new lip ring I'd gotten last week.

Zack asked, "Are you really worried about this warlock?"

I sighed. "I don't know. He may be planning something or he may just not have knowledge of my kind. There have been quite a few witches and warlocks that I've met who know nothing of the Messordei. Of course there have been many more who do know what I am and my purpose."

Zack turned right on to a private road with signs reading "Trespassers will be shot", "Beware of Dogs", - that one I felt was an understatement - and "Turn back now or Die". I personally liked the last one. Zack stopped at the large iron gates and punched in the pass code on the keypad. The gates creaked and groaned as they opened. "You need to have someone oil those."

Zack nodded his head. "I'll tell Max."

Giant wolves of various colors walked around, calmly scanning the area for danger. I looked at each of the handsome and perfectly muscled men walking around without shirts or shoes on and smiled. It was a woman's dream place to ogle men. I did love werewolves.

Zack stopped the car at the main ranch house, which was close in size to a mansion, and rushed to my door, opening it for me. The werewolf compound, or werewolf ranch as I liked to call it, sat on one thousand acres with hundreds of houses where the werewolves of the Western Valley Pack lived. Most of the houses were hidden deep in the forest where no one would ever see them though.

I hopped down from the truck, holding Zack's hand for balance, and then adjusted my shirt and pants before we started walking. A female growled from beside a building, and I lifted my lips, showing my teeth to her as Zack growled. She stayed where she was while I continued walking towards the house. I got halfway before five men blocked my path. I sniffed faces and kissed each of their cheeks as they kissed and sniffed mine. Werewolves were a very touchy-feely bunch and many of the men ran their hands along my exposed stomach and back. I felt the presence of magic and authority and turned to my right. Max walked down the steps and all of the men except Zack moved away from me. Zack took a step to the right, away from me, but stayed relatively close.

I kept my gaze even with Max's as I always did. He looked about twenty-five although I knew his real age and he was no twenty-year-old. He rested his hand against my cheek then gently nipped the end of my nose. "You missed last week."

I flicked my tongue across his cheek and fought the urge to rub my nose. "Sorry, Max."

Max hugged me against him, and we both inhaled loudly. He kept his arm around my shoulders as we walked into the house. Zack followed close behind while the others lingered behind, giving us room. The house was decorated in a western theme complete with antlers and animal heads hanging on the wall. I stared at the lion's head and wondered what werelion pride he had been from. Unlike the human's trophies, all of Max's mounted heads were from a wereanimal he had killed in war. I rubbed my nose on Max's shirt, earning me a frown and a lip twitch of disapproval. I loved to irk him.

We finally arrived to the dining room where a long, rectangle dining table, built to seat ten, sat in the center of the room. The place-settings were already set and, water was already in the glasses, even at my seat. Had he known I was coming? I moved away from him and walked to sit at the head of the table on the far wall directly across from Max's head table seat. I was the unofficial alpha female of the Western Valley Pack. I had not mated with Max, but I had the same authority as if I had. Max smiled at me as the other six men took their seats at the table. Zack took his place beside me and rubbed his knee against mine. Something was bothering him to cause him to need physical contact. I wanted to look at him, but I didn't want to draw Max's attention to it. I also knew I couldn't mind-communicate with him because Max would sense it and had an ability to tap into our conversation.

Five women began setting food down in front of us, and I stayed alert. The women despised me for my position and for taking away their most eligible bachelor. Plus, the fact that I was the only female allowed to share in the meals of the pack's highest-ranked irked them. Oh, and the fact that they all had to fight their way to the top and Max set me in my position was another matter. Not that I couldn't hold my title. I had already fought ten battles and easily won them. Did it bother me that the women hated me? Not one bit.

I cut off a piece of the steak. "Thank you, Eros, for your

protection this day and the food I am to eat. Help, protect, and advise me with this new threat." I tossed the piece of food into the air and watched as it disappeared. Everyone began talking about funny events that had happened that day, ignoring my prayer.

Luke, Max's second in command, cleared his throat. "Last night I was walking past my house when I heard Kimmy talking to a boy." Kimmy was Luke's youngest daughter at seventy-five years old. "I snuck around the corner of the house and saw Tim with his arms around her, talking real sweet to her." Tim was one of three orphans Max found fifty years ago in England. "So, I snuck up real quiet while Tim was leaning in for a kiss and yelled, 'Squirrel!' You should have seen how high they both jumped. Tim ended up hitting heads with Kimmy making her mad, and she stormed off to the house while Tim ran back home."

Everyone, including me, laughed loudly, picturing the tough warrior, Tim, jumping and bumping heads with Kimmy.

Max's number one rule for dinner was that no serious business should be discussed. I tried to look away from him, but he continued to look up at me with worry glazing his eyes. The women continued to come in and refill the drinks and replenish the plates throughout the meal. One of the women was very young looking and very attractive. I found myself watching her out of the corner of my eye. She stopped on the far side of the table, set her pitcher of water down and then twisted towards me in a rapid movement. I reached up, grabbing the hilt of the knife she'd thrown. The tip quivered an inch from my face.

I turned the knife around and used it to cut up the rest of my steak as the girl stared in disbelief at me. I cleaned the knife with my napkin and set it on the table. "You shouldn't throw knives unless you can hit your target. Plus, it is poor etiquette to throw knives at the dinner table."

Zack calmly stood up and grabbed the girl by her arm, escorting her out of the room. Max stood. "Dinner's done."

Everyone filed out of the room as I continued to eat my dinner.

Max walked towards me and spoke quietly, "Zack is waiting for you."

I ate the last piece of steak and swallowed the remaining water in my cup before standing. "I know, Max."

Max gently grabbed my arm and whispered, "You know we could fix this."

I shook my head. "No."

Max stroked my cheek making me involuntarily close my eyes. "Would it be so terrible?"

I looked over his handsome face and perfect body. He was close to five hundred now and age seemed to only improve his looks. "I'm not designed to carry children," I answered.

He smiled. "But you are designed for pleasure."

I shook my head again. "In order to be your mate, I would have to bear you a child."

He wrapped his arm around my waist, pulling me against his chest. His body heat opened my pores, and I shivered. He nipped my ear lightly and whispered, "I could change the rules." He ran one of his fingertips along the top of my butt where a human's butt crack would have started, but where instead my tail started. His other fingertip brushed the filed down horns on my head. My senses were on overload and I knew he could taste my arousal.

I pushed his chest and then kissed his cheek before backing away from him towards the kitchen. "Time to feed."

I walked quickly through the kitchen, ignoring the glares of the women and out to the back shed. Max had been trying to break me for the past century and I was not going to give in now.

Zack stood beside the shed and frowned at me. "Are you alright? What's wrong?"

I shook my head. "I just need to feed."

Chapter 7

I walked into the shed and stared at the woman hanging in the chains, beaten and bloody. "I don't know why you all insist on dying."

She snarled softly. "Screw you."

I smiled. "No thanks." I walked to stand behind her. I could feel her soul in my head and it started to make me dizzy. I grabbed a hold of her soul and absorbed it into me whispering, "Obey". Her soul fought as they all do, but none could withstand my command.

My body thrummed with power as it absorbed the magic that had lived within her and I felt rejuvenated. I felt wrinkles flatten and smiled. It was good to be Messordei, the reaper of a god.

I walked out of the shed and noticed that my skin was glowing red as it did when my magic was running high. I smiled at Zack who stared at the top of my head. "Your horns are back."

I raised my hand and touched the side of my two horns.

"Dang it." I felt my wings aching to be freed and sighed. "Tell Max I'm going to be a minute and I need clothes."

Zack tilted his head to the side for a moment then said, "Max says he'll be right out with some clothes."

I took my sword off and laid it on the ground before taking my shirt off. I then wiggled out of my pants, underwear, and bra and handed them to Zack. I closed my eyes and released my hold on my body. My tail, already free from my pants, flicked from side to side as my wings slowly slid out of my back. I cringed as the largest part slid out then sighed in happiness. I flapped my wings a few times and flicked my tail like a whip staring at the pointed end which was shaped like an arrow. Max walked out, carrying a pair of baggy sweat pants and a shirt that secured above and below my wings. He stopped to stare at me, and I smiled at him. "You should enjoy these periods because they'll be the only times you see me naked."

Max handed the new set of clothes to Zack and walked towards me. I wrapped my wings around my body and shook my finger at him, "Ah ah ah, Max. No touching." I wasn't sure why I was teasing him. I didn't normally. Maybe it was because he teased me earlier.

He ran a fingertip down one of my wings, and I whipped him with my tail. He snarled and his eyes turned to golden wolf eyes. He hated it when I caught him off guard with my tail. I held my wings tighter as he grabbed each one and pushed. I felt my wings giving in and knew he would be furious if I let him break my wings, so I pulled them back making him stumble and sliced the tip of my tail across his back cutting into his skin.

I could smell his blood and my fangs extended to just below my bottom lip. I hadn't had them when I was first turned into a Messordei, but after fifty years, they'd appeared whenever I smelled blood. Max stepped forward, snarling, and looked at my horns. "We're going to have to cut and file your horns down before you go home again."

I flicked my tail from side to side and nodded. "I know."

He stared at my bare chest for a moment before looking up at my face. "You're beautiful to me in both forms. I hope you know that."

I sighed. "I'm aware."

He stepped forward and for once my body heat matched his. He whispered, "Let me kiss you while you're in this form for once."

I shook my head and took a step back. "No."

He hooked his arms around my neck and waist, being careful to avoid my wings and pulled me against him. "Achillia," he whispered, his words tender.

I wanted to resist and yet I didn't.

"Okay," I conceded.

He was handsome and kind and one of my allies, but I knew I couldn't have anything serious with him. He wanted children, and I couldn't bear them. He kissed my lips and I stayed perfectly still. He licked down my fangs to avoid pricking his tongue on them and my eyes rolled in the back of my head as he stroked my tail. "See, that wasn't so bad."

I fought the urge to bite him and stepped back. "Please do not do that again."

He frowned. "I don't understand why you won't let yourself be happy."

I growled, "Because you could never be happy with a woman that doesn't have ovaries! It's instinctual for you to breed for children to sustain your race. I do not have that ability." I turned away from him before he could see the tears in my eyes and grabbed the shirt from Zack. He reached towards my face to wipe the tear that had escaped and I smacked his hand with my tail, cutting him. He looked down at the cut and I sighed. "Sorry." I quickly pulled the shirt on from my feet up and hooked the halter top over my head to cover my chest. Zack handed me the pants and I pulled them on just below my tail.

Max was still staring at me when I turned around, and he noticed the tears in my eyes. "Achillia—"

I raised my hand and walked away from him towards the house. "Don't."

I folded my wings around my body and squeezed through the doorways. Luckily they had been built wide enough for the werewolves while in wolf form, so I fit easily. I sat down on the floor of Max's study in front of the fireplace and folded my wings inside my back. My tail was wrapped around my waist comfortably. Max sat in his chair beside the fireplace and asked, "Where's the red wolf, Zack?"

I answered for him, "I scared him away when I came home."

Zack spoke up quickly after me, "He went crazy and trashed our place and forced me to hurt him after he hurt me."

Max glared at me. "You scared him away?"

"He was bleeding on my thirteenth century Egyptian rug!"

Max sighed. "Fine, just look for him tomorrow. If you can't get him to come calmly I will go see if I can bring him in unharmed." He looked back at me and smiled. "Your skin is tan again."

I looked down at my normal skin color and nodded my head. "The red tint only lasts for a few minutes after I absorb a new soul."

Max frowned at my horns. "It's going to hurt when we cut them."

"I know. We should get it over with soon, so I can go home."

Max continued to frown. "What's the new threat, Achillia?"

Of course he wouldn't forget. "There's a warlock at school. He didn't attack me, but I don't know if he's planning something or not. He didn't act like he should have towards me."

Max folded his arms across his chest. "You should drop out."

I blinked at him. "What? No way!"

His face went completely neutral and I knew I was sunk.

"At least let Luke look in to him for me. Maybe he's one of the warlocks who don't know about my kind."

Zack looked at Max. "Do you want me to kill him?"

I smacked Zack's arm and glared at him. "You are not killing him!"

Max eyes widened. "You're attracted to him."

I opened my mouth and then closed it. "Why does his appearance matter? He's a young boy."

Max's lip twitched and his anger began building.

I smiled. "You're jealous of a teenage boy, and all I admitted was that he was attractive. You need to go on a hunt to relieve your stress."

Max's face went neutral again as he spoke, "Zack don't kill him, yet. Luke!"

Luke walked in and bowed to Max and then dropped to a knee in front of me. "Greetings sister."

I smiled. "Hello, brother Luke."

Max cleared his throat making us both look at him. "Luke, I need you to look up a boy who goes to Achillia's school."

Luke looked at me. "What's his name?"

I frowned. "I didn't catch his last name, but his first name is Bryce and he just started at the school."

Luke smiled. "I'll find him."

I turned back to the fireplace as they began talking and remembered the first time I had sat here. Max had saved me, and since then I'd been a permanent fixture in this pack.

Max cleared his throat, pulling me from my memory. "Are you ready to go home or would you prefer to stay here?"

I looked at Zack and saw the hope on his face. "Fine, we can stay here, but I need to get rid of these horns before school."

Max shook his head. "You aren't going tomorrow. Luke won't be able to find anything until late tomorrow so you'll stay home a day."

I glared at him. "You know that I could go against your orders, right? I'm not as fragile as you like to believe."

Max's right eyebrow arched up. He was so sexy when he did that.

I sighed. "I'd like to note for the record that I'm choosing to stay home out of precaution."

Zack rushed forward and hugged me. "Thank you." He turned to Max and waited impatiently. Max nodded his head and Zack rushed from the room and out of the house. Zack wasn't home often with his pack and when he was, he used the time as best as he could.

Luke looked at my horns, and I sighed again. "You can touch them if you want, but you aren't allowed to touch my tail."

He walked forward and ran his fingertip along my right horn sending a chill down my spine and making my tail flick. Luke smiled. "You're truly a beautiful race. I find it hilarious that so many people have tattoos with depictions of your kind and don't even know what you are."

I shook my head. "Don't remind me. These humans think we're devils because that's what the stupid witches and warlocks told them. Stupid, magical humans."

Luke eyed my twitching tail, and I pulled it back around my stomach.

"It has a mind of its own sometimes."

He backed away from me as Max came towards me. "I'll go look up your warlock."

I watched as Luke walked away then looked up at Max. "You're devious. You planned this, didn't you?"

Max sat in his chair beside me and smiled. "Why would I plan anything?"

I stood and stretched my body. "Because you want something you can't have and it's driving you crazy."

He watched me as I bent down and picked up my sword. "There has to be some way to compromise."

I shook my head. "I'm not willing to compromise your position as Alpha just because you want to get me in your bed."

I fluffed my hair around my horns and looked up at him through a veil of my hair. "Could we leave my horns until tomorrow? I do miss having them."

Max moved faster than my eye could catch and pinned me to the floor. My sword was at his throat out of instinct, and he stared into my eyes. "One day you'll give in and let me take you while you're in your true form. One day you'll let me show you how truly beautiful and perfect I think you are."

I pulled my sword away from his throat and kissed his cheek. "One day perhaps. But not today."

He sat up, and helped me stand with him.

"You should go on a hunt with your pack."

Max shook his head. "I won't leave you alone at night. We'll go tomorrow morning. Will that please you?"

I shook my head. "You need to hunt with the moon. Go. I'll be fine."

Max shook his head. "Come with us."

I groaned. "You know I can't go with you. The females always try to kill me and I'm tired tonight. That one already tried to kill me today."

He frowned. "If I go you have to sleep in my bed."

I smiled. "No sex."

He nodded. "Fine."

He took my hand, and we walked out to the grassy area in front of his house. I stepped away from him as he howled loud and long. I could hear the answering yips of the pack and waited as they all came running. Ten of the men who approached first rushed to me and sniffed and kissed me in greeting. A few children who hadn't seen me with horns or a tail before stared at me in shock. Their fathers patted their backs. "She won't harm you, don't worry."

Zack jogged up and stood next to me. My faithful body-guard and pack mate. Max looked at all of the eager faces of the hundred wolves he was alpha over. "We're going on a hunt!"

The pack began barking excitedly, which sounded odd from their human throats. Zack looked at me and whispered, "Are you..."

I shook my head. "I'm staying in the house."

He sighed. "I'll stay."

I shook my head again. "No, you're going hunting with your pack. I can protect myself."

Zack opened his mouth to object, and I smacked him with my tail. "Ow," he said as he rubbed his butt cheek.

Max looked at me for a moment, then turned to the pack. "Achillia will be staying here while we hunt, since the females of this pack can't control themselves and Achillia doesn't want to kill any more of you. If there's trouble or anyone hears her call for help you are to immediately run to her aid and summon the rest of us. Is that understood?"

The pack all nodded their heads, although the women glared at me while doing it. They wouldn't call for help if I needed it. Max walked to me and rubbed his face against both of my cheeks. "Stay safe. If you need help you know how to get my attention."

I rubbed my cheek against his and nodded. "Have a good hunt."

Max started unbuttoning his pants and I ran for the house. I made it to the front steps when the first bone popping from his change began. I ran inside, bolting the door shut, then ran around the house locking all of the doors and windows before running up to Max's room and shutting and locking the door there. I wasn't afraid of being alone, I was afraid of Max coming back and finding the doors unlocked. I did however leave one random door unlocked every time just to irk him.

I turned on the enormous television and video game console and jumped onto his giant bed. Max loved video games as much as me, so we always had the latest games, and it became a challenge to see who could beat the game first. I, of course, always won.

Chapter 8

I played a few hours on the game, but my eyelids grew heavy. I turned off the console and lights and climbed into the silk sheets covering Max's bed. I fluffed up the pillow and laid down on my back with my sword on my chest. My tail was awkward for lying on my back, but I had become use to it. I closed my eyes, with my hands holding my sword across my chest, and sleep took me. The dream started like usual, with me standing in the throne hall of Eros. I turned towards his throne knowing he would appear in a moment. I waited, but he didn't come. I moved forward, closer to his throne, and then he appeared between his throne and me. "Hello Achillia."

I dropped to my knees in front of him. "Eros."

He was incredibly handsome, but that came as no surprise since he was the son of Aphrodite and Ares, but I forgot how handsome he was when I didn't see him for a while. His long blonde hair hung freely, the way I liked it, and he wore only a pair of jeans, showing off his muscular upper body.

He picked me up and caressed my cheek. "I miss you,

Achillia. I miss your face, your smell, and your laughter ringing in the halls."

I stood and rested my hand on the center of his chest. His skin was hot and it made me shiver in delight. "I miss you as well. I miss Olympus."

He pulled me against him and kissed my lips while running his hand along the top of my right arm. My skin prickled and then stung. I pulled back from him and looked at the new tattoo on my shoulder. "A tiger?"

He smiled. "His name is Ennio. Just say his name and he'll assist you."

I ran my finger down the tiger's back and heard and felt him purring. "You chose a cat on purpose!"

He ran his hand along my horns. "I am a jealous god."

"You know that I am yours, but would you have me live alone?"

He sighed. "I have already told you that I agree to your alliance with the werewolf pack due to their honoring Apollo, but I do not enjoy seeing your affection for this alpha wolf."

I ran my hand down his stomach and whispered, "I will work harder at finding the barrier's entrance, so I can return."

He smiled down at me. "I know your feelings for the wolf. Do not forget who I am. Would you prefer to stay with him?"

I stared at him. "Is this a test?"

He ran his hand down my cheek. "Just think about what you want. You are my favorite, and I want you happy. Oh, by the way, you're being attacked."

He waved as I was pulled away from him and the throne room. Attacked? I opened my eyes and found my sword pressed to the throat of a warlock whose hand was inches from my face. I kicked him back and inhaled, awakening my power. My skin glowed white and I smiled. "Trying to attack me in my sleep is very unsportsmanlike."

He growled, and fire shot from his hands towards my face. I deflected the fire with a force of wind, sending the fire back at him. He jumped to the side, and the fireball broke the window. "Max is going to be very unhappy." I opened my mouth and howled as loud as I could. I sounded nothing like a wolf, but the pack knew my sound and would know I needed help. The warlock rushed forward, pulling his sword from his side. I met his sword with my own, blocking his hit. "You cannot defeat me alone." I sliced his leg with my tail making him stumble backwards.

He growled. "Your kind needs to be destroyed. The gate shall not be opened!"

I tried to cut him with my sword, but he was a very good swordsman. "You know, I'm really tired of hearing that line."

He rushed me and tried to grab me, but latched on to my right arm, right next to my tiger tattoo. Ennio came to life, cutting and slashing at his hand making the warlock pull back. I stabbed the distracted warlock in his stomach burying my sword to the hilt in his midsection. "I will open the gate. I will let the gods through."

Zack jumped through the broken window, landing just behind the warlock. I didn't need to absorb a soul to keep my age, since I already absorbed the girl earlier, but I had a feeling I would need extra power soon and the more souls I absorbed the more powerful I became. I grasped his soul as it tried to escape. "Obey." I dropped the warlock's body as I absorbed the soul and let my wings come back out. "It does feel good to be in my natural body."

Zack frowned at the warlock. "How'd he get in?"

I shrugged. "I locked all of the doors except one in the pantry, but he wouldn't be able to get in through there."

Zack sighed. "You shouldn't try to rile him up so much."

Zack opened the bedroom door as Max walked up the steps and into his bedroom. He stared at the warlock and then glared at me. "What door did you leave unlocked this time?"

I smiled. "A pantry door."

He snarled. "Then how did he get in?"

I shrugged. "Don't look at me. I was sleeping."

Max frowned at me. "You're lying about something."

I sighed and looked down at my red hands. "I was sleeping, but Eros visited me."

Max snarled. "Zack find how he got in."

Zack bowed and then jogged out of the room. Max kicked the warlock and then looked up at me. "Did he harm you?" I shook my head. Max looked at my shoulder and his forehead furrowed. "Eros give you that?"

I nodded my head. "Additional protection."

Max snarled. "I hate cats."

"He's jealous of you being near me while he cannot be, except through my dreams."

Max walked slowly towards me until he was standing with his toes touching mine. "And yet you are faithful to the god you cannot be with."

I smiled. "Your pack is faithful to you when you are not with them."

He shook his head. "I don't mean obedient. I can tell that you love him."

"The love I have for my god is not the same type of love I have for..." I stopped myself realizing I was going to say for him. Did I love Max? I had never contemplated it before.

Max frowned at me. "You're face has an emotion I cannot

read. You must be tired. Come, let's get you to sleep. I will protect you tonight." He walked to his dresser and pulled out one of the few pairs of boxers he owned. He only wore them for my sake since the wolves preferred nudity.

I looked down at the warlock. "What about his body?"

Luke walked in and picked up the warlock's body. "I was on my way. I wouldn't make you and Alpha sleep with a dead warlock."

Max shut the door behind Luke and then turned back to me waiting. I sighed and folded my wings back into my body.

I shook my hands out trying to get the glow to go away, but I was still running high on energy from the warlock's soul. Max stood, facing away from me, and I could see the tension in his back. "How did your hunt go? I hope I didn't interrupt it."

Max shook his head. "The hunt was over when you called for help."

I cupped my hands then pushed them towards Max sending a cool breeze against his bare back. His muscles tightened, but he didn't turn around. I waited patiently as he tried to decide what he wanted to do. Slowly, my skin stopped glowing and returned to normal. I jumped up onto the bed and climbed in to the middle. "Are you ready to go to sleep? I can sleep alone if you aren't tired."

Max inhaled deeply and then let all of the air whoosh out of his lungs. He turned off the light and climbed into bed beside me. "Are you sure that you're alright?"

I nodded and snuggled up closer to him, lying on my side, facing away from him. "He didn't hurt me."

Max growled. "I want to know how one got on my property and into my house. They've brought the war to my pack now." I stayed quiet as I waited for him to tell me the real reason he was upset. He wrapped his arms around me, hugging me against him. "I was worried when I heard your call. It took all of my willpower not to rush in blind, and break down the doors. Zack told me he was close, though. So, I didn't charge in."

"I can protect myself, Max. I don't understand why you are so protective of me. I appreciate the few times you've saved me, but maybe it would be better for you and your pack if I left." It pained me to think about leaving Max and Zack, but I couldn't risk causing them trouble.

Max tightened his grip on me. "No. You're part of this pack."

I shook my head. "I'm not though. Your pack puts up with me, but I'll never really be part of your pack. I'm not a werewolf. Hell, I'm not even human, so I can't be turned."

Max bit my shoulder, and I felt his elongated canines. Only the really strong alphas could change certain parts of their body like Max. I moaned as his teeth bit farther into my shoulder. He ran his hand down the side of my body and growled softly. I tried to pull away, but he growled and held me as the infected saliva soaked into my bloodstream. The tiger on my shoulder moved into action, slicing his cheek and growling loudly. He pulled his teeth out slowly and licked the wound.

I snarled. "It won't work. I can't be turned."

He wiped his cheek where blood was dripping from the wound Ennio had inflicted. "We'll see in the morning."

I turned over and bit into his shoulder with my fangs. He growled, but let me bite him. I didn't swallow any of his blood, but let some of it trickle out as a punishment for biting me. I pulled my fangs out and let them retract, then faced away from him again. He rolled me over, onto my back, and kissed my lips fiercely. He had never kissed me in that way before. Always small light kisses, never ones that showed the need that he felt. I found my body reacting to his and before I could decipher how, he was lying on top of me with my legs on the outside of his hips. He kissed his way down my jaw and throat, stopping to lightly kiss his bite. My head was reeling with all of the things that had happened and I couldn't focus on stopping him. He ripped my shirt off, snapping the cord that fastened it to my neck and kissed his way down the center of my chest. My back arched and he nipped my stomach. "Max. You agreed no sex."

He slid my pants off quickly and nipped the inside of my thigh. "I know."

He kissed his way down my thigh, and I tried to back away. "Max."

He stopped and whispered, "Why not? It's not sex, so we aren't mating. And you are designed to enjoy this type of thing."

He wasn't wrong. "If I let you do this I might as well let you sleep with me," I grumbled.

He flicked his tongue across the center of me and I gasped.

"Yes, I know," he whispered.

Max was very skilled with his tongue and when he had finished, I felt like I was floating on a cloud in Olympus. I couldn't complete a thought and my body was so worked up that I couldn't fall asleep. I didn't want it to end, not just for my part, but for him as well. As he lay down beside me I decided to do something I never thought I would. His eyes rolled in the back of his head as I pulled him into my mouth. I could see as well in the dark as the light and I enjoyed watching his reactions as I worked to please him. Eros had said that he wanted me to be happy. As long as I wasn't mating with Max, we could all be happy. Max gripped the bed sheets as I rolled my tongue around him and ran my hand up his stomach.

He whispered my name and something inside of me clicked. I worked harder to please him and as his breathing became more erratic, I smiled. His body bucked once against the bed while his eyes were rolled in the back of his head as he finished. I moved back to lie down beside him and Max blinked at me. "You're full of surprises lately."

I laid my head on his chest, listened to the rapid beat of his heart, and smiled knowing I had caused it. For the first time, we slept together naked and it strangely felt right.

* * *

My tail was draped over Max's waist, and he gently stroked it, sending pleasant chills through my body, waking me up. "Wake up Achillia."

I opened my eyes to his smile. "Did you sleep well?"

I nodded. "Yes. Did you?"

He ran his hand up my tail and then down to cup my butt. "Yes."

I felt him grow hard against me, and my hormones began thinking for me. "Max..."

He kissed his way down my throat. "Yes?"

I pushed his chest and rolled off of the bed. "No."

"It's so much better than what we did last night. Let me show you."

I shook my head and quickly got dressed in a spare set of clothes I kept in his room for such occasions, well, not specifically this occasion. "No."

He stood off the bed and pulled a pair of jeans on then

pulled me against him, hugging me tightly. "I'm sorry. I shouldn't have brought it up. Last night was nice though."

Nice? Amazing was a better description, at least for me. Of course I had nothing to compare it to whereas Max had had a mate before. She was killed in a battle four hundred years ago. Losing her took a lot of Max's goodness away, and it was centuries before he would even think about taking another mate.

Max kissed my throat where he had bitten me yesterday and sighed sadly. "I guess you can't be turned."

I smiled. "I tried to tell you. Humans can be turned, not me."

He looked up at my horns. "We should cut those after breakfast."

"But I like my horns," I whined.

He smiled. "I like them too, but you might get a few stares when you go back to school."

"I think it would be fun to walk to school with my horns and tail hanging out."

Max shook his head and led me down the stairs by the hand. Ennio growled softly down at his hand and I ran my fingertip over the tattooed tiger, "Calm down. Eros said he wanted me happy and right now I am." The tiger purred under my touch, but I could feel the resentment towards Max touching me.

We stepped into the dining room and all of Max's closest brothers stood up. They bowed their heads in submission while Max and I took our seats at opposite ends of the table and then all of the men sat. Zack sniffed me then smiled. "Did you have a good night?"

I punched his arm making him wince. "Don't tease me."

He rubbed his arm. "I just asked a question."

The women brought in the food, giving me their best evil glares as they served me. Zack ate off my plate first so that the women wouldn't poison my food and then I began eating. Breakfast was eaten in silence for the first time since the pack war twenty years ago. I looked up at Max to see what the problem was, when I felt Luke behind me.

He grasped one of my horns and then I felt the cool metal as he snipped off my horn. I screamed in pain and gripped the arm of the chair making it crack. "Son of a...Luke!"

He ignored me, tossing the piece of my horn to Zack as he prepared to cut my other one. I held my tail between my hands so I wouldn't break the chair anymore and screamed again as he cut my other horn. "Mother...damn!"

Luke waggled my cut horn at me. "Mind if I keep this one?"

I shook my head. "No. I don't mind."

Luke set the bolt cutters on the ground behind my chair, and I glared at them before returning back to my plate of food. Zack had finished eating and walked out of the room with my horn tucked in his pocket. I stared after him and then turned to Max. "Where's he going?"

Max smiled. "He'll be back."

I frowned. "He never leaves me."

Max's smile faltered a little, but barely noticeable. "He's going to get the file for your horns. He's not leaving you."

At least ten minutes passed without Zack returning. I pushed my plate away no longer hungry and stood up. "May I be excused?"

He nodded, but I could see the curiosity in his eyes. I walked through the kitchen and out the back door and stopped in my tracks. Two warlocks had Zack pinned on the ground with a sword at his throat. I ran forward as silently as possible and kicked the sword out of the one warlock's hand while punching the other warlock in the face. They both stumbled back and Zack hopped up, growling. I pointed to the house and he howled understanding the need for reinforcements.

Another warlock ran from the side of the house pulling his pants up and I noticed a female werewolf pulling her dress down. "You traitor!" I yelled at her.

I wanted to go after her, but I had three warlocks to fight. I reached for my sword and realized that I hadn't put it on this morning. "Stupid."

I punched and kicked at the warlocks, not giving them enough time to speak as I touched them. I brought flames to my hands and covered one of the warlock's faces with it. He screamed in pain as his face melted. I tossed a fireball at the other and had enough time to ponder why Max wasn't here yet when I heard the sound of breaking dishes. Zack snapped the neck of the warlock he was fighting and then rushed over, snapping the neck of the burned warlock.

I stared at the last warlock and he smiled. "The prophecy is coming. We already know where the child is."

I tossed a fireball, but he dodged it. "Really? You wouldn't mind telling me who he is, would you?"

The warlock chanted quickly and a fireball the size of a basketball flew from his hands, making me and Zack jump out of the way. I pointed to the house and Zack shook his head refusing to leave me alone with a warlock. The warlock rushed towards me, giving Zack a perfect opening to jump on his back and snap his neck. He had underestimated Zack as a threat. Dumb move.

We looked at each other over the warlocks' bodies, then rushed inside. Max was holding a warlock up by his throat and the dark anger and hate that Max held on his face turned me on so much that I had to put my hand against the wall to keep from falling. I walked slowly towards him as he snapped the warlock's neck and dropped the body. He looked at me with golden wolf eyes and asked in a growly voice, "Are you alright?"

I nodded and kissed him on the lips, shocking him and everyone in the room. He pulled back and stared at me.

"Now I'm beginning to think something is wrong," he said.

I just smiled and then I remembered the female wolf. "I know who our mole is."

That got everyone's attention. Max's eyes, already gold, began to glow like molten fire. His voice was barely understandable as his wolf took over, but I comprehended, "Lead the way."

I walked quickly out the front door and sniffed for the female. I caught her scent by the edge of the house and followed it towards the trees. Zack stayed beside me scanning for threats to protect me from, while Max growled behind us. Ten other wolves, including Luke, followed behind him. I stopped next to a tree where she had rested and noticed the clothes on the ground. I pointed to the pile. "She's changed."

Zack sniffed her clothes quickly and growled, "Desiree."

Max looked at me. "Do you want me to summon her or would you prefer to hunt her?"

My eyes widened. "You're allowing me to decide?"

He nodded. "You're alpha female and she is female. You punish her as you want."

I looked at all of the wolves near us and was happy to see that they were all friends of mine. "Hunt," I whispered smiling.

Every man smiled and stripped their pants off in one

quick almost choreographed motion. Max's body rippled like water and then he grew taller. He had decided to take the warrior form, half-man and half-wolf, standing eight-feet-tall and a balance of man and wolf parts. Humans would have thought him grotesque or frightening, but it was beautiful to me. He nodded at me as soon as everyone was done changing. I met Zack's eyes, now one foot taller than my head. "Let's hunt."

I was the leader of this hunt and for the first time, I ran in front of the pack. I ran as fast as I knew they could and they began yipping in delight at the thought of catching prey. A rabbit darted across our path, but the wolves with me were well over one hundred years old and they knew which prey we hunted. I caught Desiree's scent to the left and dodged around a tree towards the smell. The pack followed me obediently. Max stayed silent beside me as we ran, but I could feel his excitement. I caught movement to the right and then I saw the grey she-wolf running towards the creek. "Too slow," I snarled.

I pointed and the rest of the wolves saw her. Their hackles rose, and I felt their need for blood. I ran forward with them right on my heels. Desiree was pacing at the creek deciding if she could jump it or not. Werewolves do not swim, they sink. Low body fat had its disadvantages.

I slammed into her side, and the fight was on. She sliced in to my left arm and I grabbed a hold of her jaw, pulling down and snapping it loose. It bobbed around as she growled in pain. I tried to get a hold on her, but her fur was slick and I didn't have any weapons. I backed away from her and did something she wouldn't expect. "Desiree of the Western Valley Pack you have been found guilty of treason and conspiring with the enemy. Your punishment shall be death."

I looked at the wolves snarling behind me and whispered, "Kill her." They didn't hesitate. As one, they rushed forward tearing, biting, clawing and killing the traitorous she-wolf.

Max stood beside me not partaking in the punishment. When there was nothing left, but mush and bones, the wolves looked at me, still hungry for more blood. I tilted my head to the side and Max smiled. That was frightening, in his current state. He changed down to his wolf form and I jumped on to his back as he raced deeper into the forest after more prey.

I pressed myself flat to his back as tree branches whizzed above my head. I caught the scent of the deer just before I saw the herd running. Max rushed forward, taking a doe down and with one chomp of his teeth, he ended her life. The others raced forward taking more of the herd down. Max ripped open the doe's belly and turned his head to me. It was customary for the alpha to offer his mate food first, but I was trying not to be his mate. And, yet, I also didn't want to insult him. I climbed off his back and pulled a chunk of meat off eating it quickly then backed away to allow Max his food. He didn't seem completely pleased with my portion, but the smell of the blood and meat stole his objection away. I folded my legs under me as I watched the wolves satisfy their bloodlust and hunger.

Zack finished first, jogged over to me, and lay down beside me. I stroked my fingers through his fur and felt my adrenaline depleting. I would need a nap soon. Max finished with his deer and walked over to me, lying his head on my lap. It was very uncharacteristic of him to allow Zack to be near me at the same time, but I didn't want to spoil the moment by asking. I pet Max's giant head while I pet Zack and smiled. Two of my three favorite men. Would Apollo have sat beside me while I pet them? I felt the wind pick up and smiled. No, he was another very jealous god.

The tiger on my shoulder was growling softly, but I ignored him. "This is my family so you're going to have to get used to it," I whispered softly. He didn't like the idea, but he lay down and stopped growling.

The walk back seemed to take twice as long as the run there, but I didn't mind walking in the forest. Max walked slowly ahead of me with a troubled look on his wolf-face. Zack stayed by my side and I rested my hand on his shoulder as we walked.

The house was in perfect order when we arrived and the women were nowhere to be seen. Just as well, I didn't feel like fighting anyone again. Max nudged me towards the stairs and I sighed. "Fine."

Zack whined, and Max growled softly. Not a warning or order, but still a definite, "stay here" growl. Zack flopped down on the ground with his head on his paws facing the stairs as we climbed. Max pushed me towards the bathroom and I shook my head. "No way." He licked my hand and I groaned. "I'm such a softie."

He wagged his tail and opened his mouth in a wolfish grin. Damn werewolves. I opened the bathroom door and started the bath. It wasn't really a bathtub, more of an in-floor pool. It was Japanese in style, modeled after the bathhouse Max had visited in his younger years. I arranged the shampoo and soap then tested the water. Luke warm just like the werewolves could handle. I heard Max changing back to his man form, so I stripped my clothes off and climbed into the water.

Max was sitting very still with his eyes closed as he fought the pain and gained control over his wolf. I dunked my head under the water and then washed my face with the soap while he worked things out with his wolf. As I rinsed my face, he climbed into the water slowly. His skin was still sensitive from the recent change and he grimaced as he sat down in the water. I waited a moment until I saw his face relax before squirting shampoo in my hand and moving to sit behind him. I lathered his hair up and scrubbed his scalp before touching his shoulder to let him know I was finished. He dunked his head under the water and rinsed out his hair. I picked up the wash-cloth and poured soap onto it, waiting as he finished rinsing.

We finished our bath quickly and then we hurried to the room for a nap. I wasn't the only one tired from the morning's activities. Just as I drifted off to sleep I felt cold metal against my head. "Zack…"

He began filing down my horns and smiled. "It's mid afternoon and we'll have to leave soon. I hate filing these off at home."

I turned my head and realized Max was gone. "Where'd he go?"

Zack shrugged. "He went for a walk. He looked upset."

"I hope I didn't talk in my sleep again."

Zack smiled. "Mmmm…potatoes."

I smacked his arm and sat up so he could reach my horns easier. "I was hungry and you baited me in to saying it by telling me they were on sale."

Zack laughed. "I'm so glad I got that on video."

"And then you put it up on the internet. Thanks, by the way."

He smiled. "There've been over five hundred thousand hits."

I looked up at Zack and asked something I had been

wanting to for years, "Do you think I cause too many problems for your pack?"

Zack stopped filing and looked at me. "No. Why would you ask that?"

"If I wasn't here your females would behave better—"

Zack shook his head. "No they wouldn't. They'd be attacking whoever the female Max had chosen was. They used to attack his former mate."

"I cause you more problems than you would have if I had never shown up."

Zack smiled. "It's fun, not problems."

I stood up and realized I was clothed. Max. I frowned and looked out the window at the trees. "I think I should leave." I heard the crack in my voice and fought to keep control.

Zack rushed forward and I felt his worry. "No. No, don't leave. Did I do something?"

I shook my head. "This is not my place."

He was trying to give me space, but I knew he desperately wanted to touch me. Wolves like touching to console themselves. I moved away from him and put my sword on keeping my face averted. "Tell Max that I'm sorry."

Zack wrapped his arms around my chest and hugged me. "Don't leave me. You're my pack mate. Who am I going to sleep with?"

I knew he meant actually sleep, not sex, but I smiled. "I hadn't realized we were sleeping together."

He turned me around and stared down at me. "Don't leave. The others will miss you, too."

I shook my head. "Your pack should be just that, your pack. I am not a wolf and I never could be. I need to go."

Zack reluctantly released me with a tear in his eye. "But you're my pack."

I shook my head. "I can't be part of this pack. I'm sorry. Tell Max not to come looking for me."

I pulled my tennis shoes on and walked down the stairs. Luke looked up at me, his eyes watering. I had forgotten about the werewolves' super hearing. He wiped his eyes and whispered, "The boy at your school is an orphan. He probably doesn't know about his powers."

"Thank you."

He whispered, "Don't go. Zack isn't the only one who will miss you."

"Goodbye Luke. Thank you for everything that you've done for me."

He opened his mouth to say something else, but I ran from the house. I could smell Max, which meant he was only one hundred or so yards away. I looked up in the window and saw Zack's sad face and felt my heart constrict. This family wasn't meant for me. As much as I wanted it, I couldn't stay here. I was already veering from my path. Even though Apollo had assigned Max to protect me, I needed to leave. Max didn't need to protect me any longer. I was well used to this world and could protect myself.

Zack watched me walk away a few steps then howled loudly. It was a mourning howl and Luke howled with him. Max would hear it, too, which meant I needed to leave now. I ran down the dirt road, kicking up a dust cloud behind me and heard more voices joining the howl. They were saying goodbye and don't go to me at the same time. It was heart wrenching.

"Just keep moving," I told myself sternly.

Max's smell grew stronger and I saw his shadow in the trees to my left. I increased my speed and jumped easily over the ten-foot fence, landing on my feet on the other side. Max stared at me from behind the fence's bars and whimpered. My throat constricted with emotion, and I ran. Max's howl was the most unnerving of all. His mournful howl followed me thirty miles home and echoed in my head as I shut and locked my front door.

"I had to do it." I reminded myself. "It's for the good of the pack."

I didn't believe myself, but I locked my emotions away and climbed the stairs to my bedroom. I took out the large metal file in my drawer and worked on my horns, filing them down until my hair was able to cover them. My cell phone vibrated on top of the dresser where I had left it yesterday. I looked down at the caller ID, "Max." I hit reject and collapsed on to the bed. "Eros, take me in to the dreamland."

I waited for the world to evaporate, but when it didn't I sighed. "Fine." I rolled onto my side and fell asleep the old-fashioned way, dreaming about unicorns and rainbows.

Chapter 9

School was unbearable the next day, and I fought to control my emotions and avoid killing anyone. Lunch finally came, saving me from the monotonous voice of my second period teacher. I sat down under the trees and pulled out my sandwich. "Thank you, Eros, for protecting me from the threats I encountered these past days." I laid the bite of food down on the ground and watched as it soaked through.

"That's a cool trick. How'd you do it?" asked a male voice.

I looked up into Bryce's face. "Sorry. A magician doesn't reveal her tricks."

He smiled and sat down in front of me. I was not in the mood for this.

"So, how come you weren't at school yesterday?" he asked.

I felt my tail twitch inside my pants and frowned. "I wasn't feeling well."

He frowned back. "Oh, I'm sorry. Are you feeling better now?"

I narrowed my eyes at him. "Why are you talking to me?"

His eyes widened, but his voice remained calm. "I…" He looked down at his hands. "I've always been an outsider, and I noticed that you were too. I thought maybe we could be outsiders together."

There at the tail end of his words, I smelled his arousal. Ah. "If you're looking for more than friendship I cannot offer it to you."

He smiled. "Got a boyfriend?"

My lip twitched as it tried to smile. He had no idea.

He looked at my arm and his eyebrows rose. "You got a tattoo?"

I shrugged. "Yeah."

He moved towards it and I felt the tiger growl.

I rubbed it and smiled. "Still sore."

He sat back. "That's cool. It's a really good tat. I mean the tiger looks so real. Like it could jump out and attack me."

I smiled. "That would be fun to see, wouldn't it?"

He frowned, but kept his cheery attitude. Yet another reason for me to dislike warlocks. "So, what is there to do around this town?"

I ate my sandwich halfheartedly, not feeling hungry since yesterday. "I don't know. I don't go out much." Well, except to kill warlocks.

His mouth gaped open. "What? Oh man, you need to get out. There has to be a club or something around here."

I shrugged. "Sorry, I'm not interested in that type of thing."

He tapped his chin. "What do you like to do?"

How could I answer that? Kill warlocks. Torture witches. Consume people's souls. No, none of those would work. "I stay home and read."

"You're a bookworm? I never would've guessed that. You look more like someone who likes action."

Oh, you poor ignorant boy. "I think everyone likes a little action now and then." I remembered the hunt with Max and my heart hurt. He hadn't tried to call except once and I knew he was giving me my space, but soon he'd either send Zack or he'd come visit me himself. I needed to keep them safe, even if that meant having a broken heart.

"Are you alright? You look like you're going to cry." he asked sincerely.

I closed my eyes for a second then shook my head. "It's nothing. So, where are you from?"

He smiled at my attempt to finally talk to him. "I was born in New York, but my parents died when I was two and so I've been all over the country in foster homes. I think this one will finally work, though."

The bell rang, saving me from having to continue the conversation. We walked silently towards class, and I caught him staring at Ennio. "What?" I asked.

He looked straight. "I could have sworn the tiger was growling."

I laughed. "That's ridiculous." I made a note to myself to figure out a way to punish the little feline when I got home. My nerves began increasing and I felt more magic. "Oh crap." I turned to the left and saw two warlocks moving fast towards us. "Do you know them Bryce?"

He looked at the two men dressed casually, but both carrying what looked like walking sticks. "Nope. Never seen them before in my life."

The men stopped ten feet away and smiled at me. I took a step forward so that I was in front of Bryce. "Leave here. You are not welcome."

One of the warlocks spoke to Bryce. "We're friends of your

parents. We've come to take you to those who you belong with."

Bryce shook his head. "Sorry dude, but I don't know you and I'm not going anywhere with you."

The warlock sighed. "The she-devil must have put a spell on him."

I put my hands on my hips. "I'm not a devil and I didn't put any spell on him."

The warlocks pointed their staffs at me and I formed a shield around Bryce and me. Blue sparks reflected off the shield, and Bryce gasped. "Holy crap. What's going on?"

I looked at him. "Do you trust me?"

He nodded.

I smiled. "Don't trust them. They want to take you and turn you in to a weapon to kill me."

He frowned. "Why would they want to kill you?"

I turned back to the warlocks. "I know you found your prophecy, so why don't you run along after him."

They both winced.

My eyes widened. "Well I'll be a monkey's uncle." I looked at Bryce. "Want to ditch school?"

He shrugged. "Sure, but what about those guys?"

I smiled. "How about you just follow me and then I'll deal with them?"

He nodded, and I started running. Bryce was fast like most warlocks and kept up easily with me as I ran towards the parking lot. We were almost to the car when my head began pounding with the amount of magic users nearby.

I turned around and counted ten warlocks and three witches. "Oh man, this is not good."

He looked at all of the people coming towards us and frowned. "Are they cops?"

I shook my head. "No. Bryce you have to listen to me. They want to take you and you can't go with them. I'll protect you as long as I can, but if I fail you must run and not allow them to take you."

He frowned. "You're going to protect me? I'm not incapable, you know?"

I smiled. "Against them you are. Just stay here, okay?"

He sighed. "Alright."

I stepped away from him and faced my enemies. "You will not take him. He does not want to go with you."

One of the witches stepped forward. "He belongs with others of his kind, she-devil."

"Can't you guys come up with some better insults? She-devil is so two hundred years ago."

She turned to Bryce. "This woman is not who you think she is. She's not human."

Bryce rolled his eyes. "Okay, crazy lady."

The witch frowned. "You must listen to us. She intends to kill you."

I shook my head. "Nope. Not going to kill him. You on the other hand I am going to kill." I pulled my sword from my back and heard Bryce gasp as it became visible. I rushed forward and the witch threw a confusion spell towards me. I slammed my shields up just in time to deflect her spell. The others moved forward, and I swallowed. "Are you really that afraid to fight me alone? You had to bring so many to take down one Messordei?"

The warlocks snarled in irritation.

I took the advantage to cast silence, "Tace!" I yelled. Magic came naturally to me over time, and I had increased my abilities since I'd arrived.

The few nearby warlocks and one witch glared at me as the

spell took effect. The warlocks took out their swords and I smiled. "Let's play." The sound of our blades connecting echoed in the parking lot. I killed two warlocks in a matter of seconds, but the others were casting spells one after the other and my concentration wasn't in the fight. One of the warlocks got a strike in, slicing my right arm with his sword and I groaned in pain.

I turned and saw a witch approaching Bryce who was staring at me, stunned. I tossed a fireball at her, and she caught on fire. I smiled as she ran away screaming. I blocked one of the warlock's swords and then felt immense pain in my leg. I looked down to find a sword all the way through my leg and the warlock holding it, smiling at me. I grabbed the warlock and head butted him, making him stumble back. I pulled the sword from my leg and limped backwards. The warlocks smiled at me and I backed towards Bryce. "Run."

He frowned down at me. "They hurt you?"

I looked down at my bleeding leg. "I'll live, but you need to run before they—"

I never got to finish my sentence. Darkness consumed me and my chances of survival plummeted.

* * *

Eros was frowning down at me where I was lying on the ground in his throne room. "You have some explaining to do."

I sat up and frowned. "Where am I?"

He sighed. "The warlocks have captured you. Why were you guarding a warlock boy?"

I winced when I tried to stand and saw my leg. "Crap. Eros, he's the prophecy the warlocks kept talking about. The one who can open the door. If I can convince him to help me, then we can open the door."

Eros let it sink in for a moment then smiled. "I knew there had to be a reason that you were protecting a warlock. It's not natural for you to be protective of them."

"Did you think I was betraying you? I could never betray you. I am your pawn, your servant."

He stroked my cheek and smiled. "I know, Achillia. Oh, you should wake up. They're about to start torturing you. Remember Ennio is there if you need him."

I jolted awake just as a warlock stabbed my other leg. I screamed in pain and heard Bryce yelling, "Leave her alone! She hasn't done anything."

If only he knew. I glared at the warlock as he pulled the sword from my leg. "Your soul is as good as mine," I whispered angrily.

He shook his head. "You won't be absorbing any more warlock or witch souls."

He grabbed a nearby man who looked to be about fifty and held him out to me. He was a Messordei like me. He looked into my eyes and asked, "Who's are you, Sister?"

I swallowed. "Eros' and you, Brother?"

He smiled. "I'm Erebus'. I offer myself to you."

I looked over and saw Bryce staring at me. I swallowed. "I hope to avenge you my brother."

He tilted his head to the side and my fangs popped out as I began absorbing his soul. Bryce gasped, but I didn't stop to look at him. The soul was more potent than any I had absorbed before. I smiled realizing how powerful he was. If I could absorb his soul I would be close to unstoppable. I was halfway through my drink, when the warlock pulled him away from me. I snarled at the warlock and then noticed Bryce's shocked face.

"What are you?" he asked.

I let my fangs retract. "That's a very long story, but I'm not a threat to you. We're both outcasts, remember?"

He frowned. "They told me that you wanted to kill me."

I laughed. "Of course they did." I shook my head. "I wouldn't kill you. Now these guys, I would kill."

The warlock smiled and pointed to my healed legs. "Looks like you need another reminder." I tried not to scream, but as he stabbed my right leg he turned the sword and I couldn't hold it in.

Bryce yelled, "What do you want with me? If I help you will you leave her alone?"

I shook my head. "No. Bryce, don't listen to them. They'll kill me no matter what you do. You can't help them."

The warlock yanked the sword from my leg and punched me in the face, knocking me out again.

* * *

I lost track of the number of days that passed after that. Bryce was taken to another room, and I tried my hardest to break free, but my beatings continued with only sips of the soul from my fellow Messordei to keep me alive. I had to think of a way to escape, but with no magic available, I was at a loss to figure out how.

A witch I had never seen before walked down the stairs carrying a tray of assorted torture devices all with shiny, pointed ends. She smiled. "Good evening, she-devil."

I growled. "Let me go, and I'll spare your life."

She laughed. "You're always so sweet." She grabbed what

looked like an ice pick off the tray and stabbed it in to my left shoulder.

I held in my scream and glared at her. "I retract my previous offer." I muttered angrily. Ennio growled on my shoulder, and I sighed. If only I had enough magic, I could release Ennio.

The witch left the ice pick in my shoulder and looked at her goodies, trying to pick her next one. A loud scream from upstairs made us both look up, as if we could see through the concrete to what was happening. She grabbed a dagger and stabbed it through my thigh and into the wood. "You've killed a lot of my family and friends, she-devil."

I ground my teeth together and whispered, "I'll kill a lot more before I die, too."

She grabbed a device that was twisted metal and jammed it through my right forearm. I screamed loudly and glared at her. "Your time will end soon." She grabbed a bat that was lying on the ground from my earlier torture and hit me in the face with it, knocking me out.

* * *

Being knocked out so many times was really starting to piss me off. I could hear snarling and growling and smelled wolf, but knew I had to have been imagining it. I opened my eyes and found myself staring at the dead witch on the ground in front of me. Strange, she was alive the last time I saw her. I looked up slowly, and painfully, and saw Max fighting with another warlock. Max was in warrior form, and the warlock didn't stand a chance. Max slashed the warlock with his clawed hand, cutting the warlock's throat open. He growled at the dead warlock before turning to me.

I swallowed the tears of joy I had and asked, "How'd you find me?"

He smiled. "Tracking device." Or at least that's what it sounded like from his snout-mouth. He walked towards me and his body rippled until he was in human form. He looked at all of the metal sticking out of me and growled. "I should have made her suffer."

I smiled, despite the immense pain I was in. "You always know just what I want to hear." I screamed as he pulled the ice pick out of my shoulder, and he stopped moving. I breathed through the pain and looked up at him. "You have to take them out. Except the one in my arm is twisted, so I'm not sure how you can get it out."

He examined the device and sighed. "I'll have Luke help." It was almost impossible for an alpha to cause females pain. Killing them quickly was one thing, but pulling things out of me and making me scream in pain each time would be too much for Max to bare.

I looked at his worried face and whispered, "I didn't think I would make it out of here."

He placed his hand against the side of my cheek that wasn't bruised and whispered, "I will always come for you."

Luke jogged down the steps in to the room and his eyes widened in shock at me. "Holy crap. Did they think you were a voodoo doll?"

I laughed in spite of everything and smiled at him. "Could you help out?"

He inspected the twisted device and somehow managed to get it out without ripping my entire arm into pieces. He worked quickly to get the rest out while Max snarled behind him. Max snapped the metal restraints holding me and picked me up in his arms. "Let's find a warlock for you to eat."

I leaned my head against his chest and whispered, "You sure do know how to sweet talk a girl."

The other Messordei looked up from the ground. "Sister."

I looked down at him and smiled. "You're free Brother."

He smiled and ran from the room. I remembered Bryce and looked up at Max, groaning from my quick movement. "Max there's a teenage boy here. He's a warlock, but he's not one of them. He's my key to the door. I need to find him before your wolves kill him."

He frowned. "The boy that Luke looked up?"

"Yes."

Luke smiled, "He's fighting Zack right now."

Max rushed out of the room and down five hallways before coming to a large dining room. The tables were smashed in to pieces and the chairs were thrown around the room. Zack stood in warrior form snarling at Bryce. Bryce was glowing and had a shield around his body. He'd learned a lot in the days I had been locked up here. Zack started to rush towards Bryce and I jumped from Max's arms, running as best as I could with my injured legs and collapsed on the ground between them. So much for graceful. "Zack. Bryce. Stop fighting."

Bryce looked down at me and frowned. "You know them?"

I nodded my head. "Yes, they're allies."

He glared at me. "They showed me what you are and explained what you do."

"I knew they would. Look, Bryce, I do kill warlocks and witches, but I wouldn't harm you. I need you to help me."

He frowned, "Help you open the door so the gods and goddesses can come back and kill all of the humans?"

I blinked at him. "They aren't going to kill the humans."

His frown eased a little, "They said you would kill them all."

I shook my head. "No. Most will become slaves, but we aren't going to kill them."

Bryce frowned. "Slaves? You can't do that."

Max growled. "Enough, let's get out of here. Achillia is badly injured, and my patience is thin."

Bryce looked at Max in all his naked glory. "Who the hell are you?"

Max snarled and I tried to stand up. My leg buckled from under me and Zack picked me up in his arms. "Achillia, I'm sorry."

I flicked my tongue across his cheek. "I need a soul."

Bryce frowned. "How can you do that?"

I looked at him and asked, "Lick his cheek?"

He glared at me. "Kill people and take their souls!"

I shrugged. "I need them to stay young. It's how the gods designed me." He backed away and I sighed. "Please, Bryce. I need your help."

He shook his head and ran away. Luke started to go after him, but Max grabbed his shoulder. "Let him go."

Luke handed me my sword and I strapped it across my back.

Zack walked me over to Max and held me out. Max took me and cradled me against him. "You've aged."

I groaned. "How much?"

Zack whispered, "Two years."

I sighed. "Son of a...I hate warlocks. Max, I need—"

He kissed my lips stopping the words from my mouth. I couldn't move or breathe and stared at him in shock as he pulled back from the tender kiss.

Pain filled his eyes. "Don't ever leave me again."

I looked down. "It's better if I leave. Look at what you've had to do already today."

He walked towards the exit, and Luke and Zack fought off the few warlocks that came near. "I would slay ogres and trolls everyday as long as you stayed in the pack."

"I miss the trolls. They made wonderful soups."

Zack caught a warlock, and Max set me down in front of him. I smiled at the warlock's angry face. "You should have killed me when you had the chance." I drained him slowly enjoying the taste of his soul. My horns grew out, my skin started glowing, and my wings expanded, ripping the back of my shirt, but luckily it stayed attached to the front.

I felt all of my wounds heal and then the power and energy left me as fast as it had come. I dropped to my knees and my wings retracted by themselves. Max picked me up and whispered, "Let's get you home."

The run back was slow due to the wounded wolves with us. Max assured me that only volunteers came on the mission and I shouldn't feel bad about them being hurt. We finally made it back to the ranch and all of the women stood outside the house glaring at us. Max's anger began building at the sight of the defiant women. "What is this?"

The women all looked at me. One stepped forward and spoke. "We want her to leave. She is not pack and has no reason to be here. She is endangering us and our families. She's a threat to all of us!"

Max set me down on the ground, and Zack rushed over, putting his arm around me so that I wouldn't fall. Max walked towards the women, and I smelled the fear on them. He spoke calmly, "The last time I checked, I was alpha of this pack. I decide who is a threat and who is not!" His calm was cracking.

"Achillia is no threat to this pack and the next female that insinuates otherwise, will be harshly disciplined."

A younger female, obviously newly-turned, walked forward. "Why hasn't she mated with you then? Perhaps you should let her fight?"

I laughed, and they all looked at me. I shook my head. "You waited until I was at my weakest to do this. That was smart planning on your part, but you are all too young to remember my previous battles. There's a reason no one before you challenged me again. If you want to fight me, wait until I'm fully healed. I'll kill every single one of you."

The young female smiled. "A true alpha female can protect her position at any time."

I pulled my sword out and sliced the female's head off in one quick motion. The swing of my sword made me stumble and I dug the blade into the ground to right myself. The woman's body fell in the grass and the women watched her head roll away. I inhaled deeply, and then looked at the women. "Anyone else want to challenge me?"

Before I could react a female ran at me from the side. She tackled me to the ground and knocked my sword out of my hands. I let my fangs extend and bit into her neck making her scream. She rolled away from me, and I stood, cringing at my soreness. "I really hate women." Five of the women started to move towards me, and Max growled. I shook my head. "Let them come. I will kill you all."

Max stepped back, but I could see his concern on his face. Zack voiced his worry. "You aren't properly healed and you're exhausted."

I smiled. "Don't worry. I've got something up my sleeve."

I backed up until we were in the open grassy area and away from the men. The five women snarled at me and started changing shape. I whispered, "Ennio." My arm burned and then Ennio jumped from my skin, landing on the ground in the same size as he'd been in tattoo form. I groaned. "Really? Eros, what is this?"

The women, all in their wolf forms, started towards me and Ennio. I sighed, "Nice knowing you."

The first woman jumped, and Ennio exploded outwards until he was twice the size of the women. Canines were no match for a feline their size or bigger and in a matter of seconds, Ennio defeated all of the women. He turned towards me, and I pet his face. "You're a good boy. Eros was very thoughtful."

Ennio turned towards Max and growled once before shrinking back down and scrambling up my pants and shirt and back to my arm.

Max snarled, "I hate cats."

I took a step and collapsed on the ground. Max rushed forward and picked me up. "I think you should rest now."

I frowned. "I shouldn't have attacked them. Now you don't have many females left."

Zack shook his head. "We have enough females and we can always find more."

The females that hadn't attacked me, quickly left the area. I looked up at Max and whispered, "They're right."

He walked into the house and up the stairs. "No. They're not. You're part of this pack and have been for two hundred years."

He laid me down on the bed, and I shook my head. "None of the females will ever accept me as part of the pack, and the only reason the men do is because I don't boss them around."

Max pulled off his pants and grabbed a baby wipe from the container on his desk. He wiped the blood off of his chest and face and tossed the wipe in to the garbage before turning around to me. "Do you want to leave?"

I stared at him in silence for a moment. "No. I don't want to."

He shrugged. "Then what's the problem. You don't want to leave and I don't want you to leave. So, who cares about the rest?"

"You're not thinking thoroughly about this, Max." I pulled my sword off, rolled over to my side and set it on the ground beside the bed. I pushed my pants down in the back just enough to slide my tail out.

Max climbed onto the bed beside me and wrapped me up in his arms. "All I can think about is the anger I felt at finding you hurt and bleeding."

I lifted myself up on one arm and looked at my new face in the mirror. "Well it's not that much different, but I don't want to get any older."

He pulled me back down and kissed my lips. "I wanted to tear them apart, limb from limb, for what they did to you."

I could see the anger building and gold specks began filling his eyes. I asked, "So, how did you find me again?"

He ran his finger across my right shoulder where I had been stabbed when he found me, "We put a tracking device inside of you."

I wanted to be mad, but instead I felt happy. "Why?"

He smiled. "Well, back then, I was worried that you would run off and tell people about us, but…"

I asked, "But what?"

He sighed. "But… Over time, I've realized that I did it because I love you. I loved you then like any dominant loves a submissive."

I rolled onto my other side flicking him with my tail in the process. "I see."

He groaned. "Achillia."

I asked, "What about your pack? Your pack is—"

Max interrupted me, growling. "My pack is my pack and not of your concern at the moment. You need to rest and you can't do that if you keep talking."

I raised one finger. "One more question. How did you know I was in trouble?"

He turned very serious and whispered, "I felt your pain at one point and then I sent Zack home to try to talk to you. When he found that you hadn't been there, we activated your tracking device."

"I wonder if I'll be able to find Bryce again before more warlocks do?"

Max wrapped his arms around me warming up my body. "Go to sleep, Achillia or I'll make Luke drug you."

I sighed and closed my eyes. "Stubborn wolf."

Chapter 10

I rested at Max's ranch for three days, only leaving his room to eat and use the bathroom. My strength had returned in the morning, but Max was worried the warlocks would try to attack me after we had killed so many of their kinds. The women no longer gave me looks, but instead treated me as they did the men. I finally convinced Max to let me go to school and stood in the center of the trees on my lunch feeling for Bryce.

I had almost lost hope when I felt him coming towards me. He walked from the side of the nearest building and my jaw dropped. He had aged three years, himself, and he looked amazing. He kept a neutral face as he walked up. "Achillia."

I rolled my tongue back up inside my mouth and smiled. "Hi, Bryce. I was afraid that you weren't going to be here."

He sighed. "I wasn't sure myself until I stepped off the bus. We need to talk."

I nodded my head. "Yes, we do."

He looked at me and asked, "Are you feeling well?"

"Yes, why?"

"They hurt you pretty bad."

I smiled. "I heal very fast. One of the perks of my creation."

He looked around and shook his head. "Do you have a car we can take and go talk somewhere?"

I nodded. "Yeah, come on."

He walked quietly beside me and I felt his nervousness.

I whispered, "I promise I would never harm you. I haven't lied to you about anything."

He nodded. "I'm not nervous about you. There've been others following me."

I smiled evilly. "Let them come. I'm ready this time."

He shook his head. "I don't want you hurt because of me. They hurt you enough before."

I stopped next to my car, and he touched my face. "You've aged like I have. Why?"

"I can choose what age to stay at, but if I am hurt too badly or do not take the measures necessary to keep that age, I progress. I can't move backwards though, only forward."

He shook his head. "Let's go so you can explain it all from the beginning."

We climbed in to my car and I drove to my house. Bryce climbed out and frowned. "You live here?"

I nodded. "When I'm in school, I live here with Zack."

He frowned harder. "The one I was fighting?"

I nodded again. "He's my protector. Please try to get along. He was only trying to protect me."

Bryce nodded. "Fine."

We walked up the steps, and Zack threw open the door snarling. "What...Oh sorry. I just smelled magic."

I smiled. "It's alright, Zack. You remember Bryce."

Zack nodded. "Sorry about the other day. I thought you were one of the warlocks that had hurt her."

Bryce smiled and held up his hands in a surrendering gesture. "No harm done."

We walked inside, and Zack brushed his hand along my arm as I walked by, marking me with his scent. I shook my head at the possessive gesture, but kept quiet. I led Bryce to the living room and sat down in the beautiful blue chair-and-a-half that Max had purchased for me last year. I had been eyeing it at the local furniture store and with a hint from Zack, Max purchased it for me as a Christmas present. I know, I know, me celebrating Christmas? Well, I celebrate the birth of my god on that day even though he wasn't actually born on that day, just like the Christians. They all know he wasn't actually born in December, but that's the day they chose to use, and I liked the tradition of exchanging gifts with friends. Besides, Max required that I spent every holiday with the pack, as part of their tradition.

Bryce sat across from me in the recliner and said, "Alright. Tell me everything."

Zack set two drinks on the table before squeezing in to the chair-and-a-half with me. I would have argued, but he was feeling threatened with Bryce there so I rearranged myself until we were comfortable and began.

"There are twenty-four gods and goddesses. Their names and duties are not important so I won't bore you with those details. Each god or goddess was allowed to create servants for themselves. Those servants helped in the policing of the humans. Humans with magic abilities are called witches and warlocks. The witches and warlocks joined together and decided that they didn't like the gods and goddesses being so close to this world and being able to walk among them at their leisure. Quite a few demigods were created by the mating of a god or goddess with a human and the demigods got a little out of control. So, the warlocks and witches figured out a way to create a barrier that blocked the gods from visiting the humans.

"The gods, of course, were upset and so they decided to create a being whose purpose is to break the barrier that separates them from the humans. Which is why I was created. The gods must use three bones from a human to create us, but even I don't know the exact details of that. I was made from the bones of Achilles, the great warrior, which is why the god that I serve named me Achillia, Daughter of Achilles. Then, after passing tests, I was turned into what I am today. We are called Messordei, which means Reaper of God. Although we serve one god specifically we are the servants for all of the gods."

Bryce asked, "What abilities do you have?"

"Immortality, super speed, enhanced hearing, quick healing and a few other things I prefer not to talk about."

He absorbed that information then asked, "What about you aging?"

"I can choose to age normally as I wish, but in order to keep a certain age I must absorb one soul every week. If I am badly wounded I must absorb a soul to heal. And sometimes, like at the warlocks', if I am wounded badly enough I age rapidly. I can die, but not from old age or diseases. I will stop aging at what appears to the human eye as fifty."

"How old are you?" he asked warily.

"I am old. I've been in this realm for two hundred years, but I was alive for many years before that in Olympus."

His eyes bulged as he stared at me. "You're over two hundred years old?"

I nodded. "I've been searching for the door to the barrier since I was turned into a Messordei. It's within one hundred miles of this exact point, but I cannot locate it. That's where you come in."

"Me? What do I have to do with any of this?"

"You are the prophesized child to end the war. You will either help me and the gods, or destroy me and my kind."

"Why should I help you?" he asked, crossing his arms over his chest.

I smiled at the defensive movement. "The warlocks told you that we wanted to kill all of the humans, but that is not true. During the times that the gods walked among the humans, everything was peaceful and good. There were no diseases, no poverty, and no starving nations. The gods took care of those that worshipped them."

"What if we don't want to worship a god?" His brows furrowed.

I shrugged. "They won't kill you or anything like that, but you won't be under their protection. Say a monsoon is coming your way. If you are under one of their protection they will avert the monsoon, but if you aren't under their protection they will leave it be. And I called them slaves before, but that was a little harsh. Humans are only required to give small acknowledgements to the gods during meals. I do it every time I eat, for example."

His eyes widened again. "That's how the sandwich melted into the ground."

I nodded. "My thanks to my god for protecting me. I give him a portion of my food and he allows me to have another meal and sometimes grants me one desire or wish."

He shook his head. "This is so much to take in. I don't understand how I am supposed to help you though. I'm not saying I'm going to. I'm just asking."

I shrugged. "I don't know either. I just know that the

prophesized child will assist me in finding the door and breaking the spell."

He stood and ran a hand through his hair. "I need time to think. Do you have a number I can reach you at?"

Zack handed him a piece of paper that had been in his hand since he sat down. "That's her cell phone number and mine under that in case you get in trouble. The others are looking for you and will stop at nothing to keep you away from Achillia."

Bryce nodded and started towards the door.

I called to him, "Bryce, I'm really not a devil. My kind is depicted as the devil because the warlocks didn't want others to see us and think we were good. They drew our images and told stories of the devil with horns and a tail. We don't kill humans or take their souls, only warlocks' and witches', and only the ones that attack us first."

He nodded again, then walked out the door.

Zack patted my arm. "You did all that you could. Now we just have to wait and see what his response will be."

"I have a feeling that we won't be able to wait that long."

* * *

I decided not to go to school anymore and stayed at the house with Zack. He sparred with me during the day, and we taught each other moves the other didn't know. By the second night, my skin was crawling, and I couldn't take it. "I need to get away from the city." I told Zack at dinner.

He looked up from his steak and frowned. "What's wrong?"

"There are a lot of magic users in the area, and I feel itchy. I can't stand it anymore. I need to get out of the city."

Zack set his fork down and opened his cell phone without another word from me. He waited patiently as the phone rang. My enhanced hearing let me hear both sides of the phone conversation. Max picked up on the fourth ring sounding agitated, "Max."

Zack talked quickly, "Achillia and I are coming to the ranch. She needs a place to sleep for a few nights."

Max's voice was worried as he asked, "Is she hurt?"

Zack shook his head then smiled. "No. We'll explain when we get there, but I don't want to delay."

Max spoke a little louder, knowing I could hear him, "Come straight here and pack heavy. I'll be waiting at the gate."

He hung up, and Zack smiled at me. "You're the only one he meets at the gate."

I rolled my eyes. "That's because he's overprotective since I'm not a werewolf."

Zack rolled his eyes back at me. "Right. That's the reason. Come on. We need to pack and get there."

We both left the dishes on the table and hurried up the stairs to our rooms. I packed one duffel bag full of clothes and necessary toiletries and then packed the other bag full of weapons. Over the two hundred plus years of my life, Ares has gifted me with many different weapons. I wore the sword only because it stayed invisible to human eyes, not because it was my favorite.

I walked quickly down the stairs, carrying one bag on each arm and out to the garage. Zack already had his bags loaded and was waiting in the driver's seat. I tossed my bags in the back of his truck and climbed in the cab. "Alright. Let's go."

Zack stayed still, not moving. I turned to him and only upon seeing the blank expression in his eyes did I smell the scent of death in the truck. I stared in shock at the black dagger sticking out of his chest and the note taped to the front of it. Tears leaked down my face as I moved slowly across the truck's cab to pull the note off of the dagger. I held my breath as I listened for any sign of life from Zack, but I knew from his soulless eyes and smell that he was dead. A single strike to the heart wasn't enough to kill a werewolf so I sniffed the dagger. I jumped back at the smell of death magic on the dagger and bit back my scream. I turned my attention to the note, holding in my emotions until I figured out who had done this.

The note was written elegantly and smelled of magic itself.

You and Max have always wanted a war, so let's have one.
I can't wait to slice your head off.
~Richard

An image of the warlock I had fought when I was only on Earth for one hundred years flashed in front of my eyes. Richard wasn't just a warlock, he was a warlock bitten by a werewolf, giving him long life, quick healing, and extra magic. Our fight lasted three days in the middle of a field in Scotland. He was a new werewolf then, which had given me the edge I had needed to keep up, but I had still been unable to defeat him. On the third day I was barely able to walk and with a chance blow, he knocked my sword from my hand. He backed me to the edge of a cliff and smiled. "You put up a good fight, but your kind should not exist. Let me end the misery that your life would be once and for all."

As he brought his sword up for the killing blow I smiled at him. "No thanks, Dick. I live well in misery." I jumped backwards flipping over as I dove straight in to the ocean. Richard's scream penetrated even the depths of the ocean as I swam. With so little energy I ended up floating and letting the ocean take me where it would. I had nightmares of him for years afterwards. He was more powerful now, and I had to kill him. Not just for me, but for Zack's soul.

I exhaled, then turned to Zack's body and began searching for any scent that I could use to trace back to the warlocks. Richard wouldn't have left a scent, but I doubted he had come here himself. He wouldn't have wanted to take the risk of having to fight me yet. I finally caught the scent and my anger and sorrow boiled up around me. I screamed and my skin started glowing. I let all of the pain I was feeling be heard, and then my scream changed to a howl loud enough it would go for miles. I couldn't touch Zack anywhere except his face until the pack came, so I kept my hand on his cheek as tears leaked from my eyes. I screamed and howled again and climbed out of the truck. I grabbed my bags and tossed them out the front of the open garage door. I could hear the distant howl of Max, and knew he would be here soon. He heard my call. My skin was glowing light blue, but I didn't care if any of the humans saw me or not. I couldn't control the color my skin glowed and it often turned a shade I'd never seen before. Blue was a new shade.

I sat down on my knees and cried for the loss of my best friend. We didn't just live together; we were pack mates. When we stayed at the house, we always slept in bed together to keep warm. He was my assigned protector, but over time, we had developed a friendship that I never knew I could have. My heart hurt at the loss of him and I knew I wouldn't be the same. I couldn't be the same without seeing his sweet smile and hearing his jokes.

A truck stopped in front of the driveway and I didn't bother to look up as I smelled Max and felt his fury. Four sets of legs rushed past me and into the garage. Max walked back and knelt in front of me, pain pinching the side of his eyes at the loss of his pack brother. "What happened?" he asked quietly.

I handed him the note and whispered, "I should have stayed away from your pack."

Max read the note then looked at me with golden wolf eyes. "This is not your fault."

I laughed bitterly. "If I had moved away from you like I should have this wouldn't have happened. I can't see how this isn't my fault. I called you for Zack and to warn you that the sorcerer who wrote that note is a werewolf. I don't know if he has a pack or if he is part of one, but he may come after yours. I'm going to go after him so hopefully he won't be able to come after you. If I don't succeed in kill—"

Max put his hand over my mouth stopping me from talking. "Shut up, Achillia. I know you're hurting, but you can't go on a suicide mission. Zack wouldn't have let you go and neither will I. You'll come back with us and we'll meet him together as a pack." I shook my head, but he kept his hand on my mouth. "For once, just do as I say. Let us help you avenge Zack."

I wanted to argue, but he was right. Zack would never have let me go off on my own. He would have followed me. I nodded and Max pulled me in to his arms. I let the tears resume and hugged Max back. One of the other wolves howled his grief, and Max and I joined in. I know I didn't sound like a wolf as the others did, but it felt right to join them in our shared grief.

Max picked me up in his arms and carried me to the SUV, while Luke grabbed my bags and put them in the back for me. We left the others to clean up the scene and Luke drove us to the ranch. Max rubbed my arms as Luke drove and hummed softly. The air was thick with grief and my heart felt like a hole had been ripped out of it. I closed my eyes and inhaled Max's scent. I had never been able to figure out what Max's distinct scent smelled like. All of the wolves smelled like the forest and wolf fur, but beneath that was their own smell. Max smelled manly. That was the only word I could use to describe him. Not like sweat, but warm and manly.

The vehicle stopped, and Max climbed out, holding me against him. I didn't open my eyes even after he lay me down on the bed. I knew I couldn't sleep, but I couldn't sit and think about Zack either. Max lay down beside me, spooning his body around mine, and stroked my hair. He didn't speak because there was nothing that could be said. All we could do was prepare for the battle that was about to happen. I rolled over and looked at Max's golden wolf eyes in his human face. "If I run, you'll track me, won't you?" I asked softly.

Max nodded, and then licked the tear tracks on my face. "Yes."

I closed my eyes and sighed. "I need to communicate with Eros and see if he has any tricks up his sleeve. Would you stay with me until I wake up?"

Max kissed my cheek and settled in against me. "I'd stay forever for you."

It wasn't the answer I was looking for, but it worked. I thought hard about Eros and relaxed into the bed. The darkness behind my eyelids grew and then I was lying beside Eros on his giant canopy bed. He stroked my cheek softly and smiled. "Hello, Achillia."

I tried to smile at him, but my grief was too new. "Hello, Eros. I haven't been here in a while."

"I am sorry for the death of the wolf friend. It pains me to feel your grief."

I nodded. "Thank you. Do you know why I'm here?"

He scowled at me. "Achillia, do not forget who I am."

I bowed my head submissively. "No offense meant, Eros."

"I do have some 'tricks up my sleeve' as you said. The one you are going to be fighting is strong, stronger than any we've encountered before. If that boy doesn't assist you, I am afraid this will be your last fight."

"I know," I agreed.

He sat me up and ran a fingertip over Ennio, who purred happily. "I have more like him to help, plus a few others. This isn't going to feel nice, but hold still and feel free to scream." He ran his hands up and down my arms and fire burned against my skin. I tried to hold in my scream, but like he said it didn't feel nice. I screamed until my throat was hoarse and my body felt numb. Eros finished just in time to prevent me from blacking out and carried me to a mirror. A bear and rhinoceros now sat on my right arm. Eros whispered, "Speak only Ennio's name and he will call the others to assist you. They will all do your bidding and will not harm your pack of wolves, unless you tell them to. I've also added a charm to increase your magic, but don't use it until you need to. To activate it touch your belly button."

Eros always liked belly buttons. It's weird, I know, but I thought it had to be because he didn't have one. I smiled and said, "Thank you. You're a very gracious god."

He kissed my cheek. "Kill the bastard and open the gate."

I woke up with Max growling over me.

I frowned at him. "What's wrong?"

He pointed to my new tattoos with a frown.

I whispered, "Gifts from Eros. Don't worry they won't harm you."

He ran his hand down my arm and the animals made noises, but none harmed him as Ennio had before. He frowned. "You smell like a barn now."

"Thanks."

He kissed my cheek and ran his hand along my tail which was lying across my stomach. "What do you want me to do?"

I stared at him. "What do you mean?"

He smiled. "Do you want the pack to assist you against this guy or do you want us to stay back?"

I wanted him to stay back so that he wouldn't get hurt, but I knew he couldn't do that. I also knew that if I accepted his assistance it would be another step of accepting him as my mate. Could his mind or his wolf's mind be changed once they chose me as their mate? I didn't want to hurt him and yet... "There isn't anything I can say to you. If I tell you to stay back, you will, until you see me get hurt and then you and your pack will jump in. Besides the battle is going to be brought here, and I'm pretty sure another wolf pack will be here. I know your pack won't want to miss that."

He inhaled. "The thought of battle arouses you. Interesting."

I growled. "You need to get the children away from here. Send them to one of your allies. I'd send the women with them as protection—"

He growled and rolled on top of me. "I can take care of my own pack."

His eyes were golden wolf eyes and there was barely a trace of humanity in his words. I dropped my eyes from his and whispered, "No offense meant. Just a suggestion, not an order."

The kiss caught me off guard since he was angry, but his lips were soft. When he pulled away, my heart was beating three times its normal speed. His eyes had thankfully returned to the hunter green shade of his human self, and he whispered, "Let's prepare for battle."

The first step I thought was odd, but I followed his orders to keep him docile and we walked to the bathroom. He turned on the tub and stripped slowly out of his clothes. If my pulse hadn't already been hammering a mile a minute it would have picked up. His tanned skin glistened in the overhead lights and his muscles were tight with his anger. I stripped quickly out of my clothes and looked down at the new tattoo of a sun around my belly button. Cute, Eros. It was strange that he used a sun since that only made me think of Apollo, the Sun God.

The tub finally finished filling and we climbed in, not looking at each other's faces. We wet our hair and then I lathered him up with soap.

He came up from under the water and his golden wolf eyes startled me. He should have been in complete control by now. I held my ground, but knew he could smell my fear. He whispered, "Whether you sleep with us or not, you are our mate."

Oh, great. He was speaking in plural now. I smiled. "Mr. Wolf, I cannot be your mate unless I bear you children, which, as you know, is not possible."

Mr. Wolf smiled. "We do not need any more children. We

had ten with our last mate. The need to bear offspring is not present anymore."

I folded my arms over my chest. "What if I don't want to be your mate?"

He moved so fast that I didn't even hear the water move. He held me against the side of the tub and whispered, "We can smell your arousal. We could smell it when you caught us strangling the warlock a few days ago, and again when we rescued you, and again when—"

I interrupted him, getting his point. "Why are you doing this?"

Mr. Wolf whispered, "Because our pack is becoming divided. We need you to proclaim your status as my mate or we won't be able to unite them."

"I need to think about this."

Mr. Wolf growled. "You've been thinking about this for fifty years."

He was right. I'd been delaying this decision far too long. I'd been focused on helping the gods, fighting the witches, and really I was just a pawn. I wanted to be free. I wanted to love and be loved.

Despite everything that was going on. and everything that had happened, I loved Max and it was time for us to be together.

I spread my legs and nodded. "You're right. It's time we became mates."

He pushed himself inside of me and I lost my voice. He was not gentle, but it wasn't painful either. There were no kisses or sweet words as I had imagined my first time with Max would be, but then again, Max wasn't in control right now. I felt the warmth and pleasure rising in me as he found his rhythm and I screamed in delight as it peaked and spilled over. His body began to lose its rhythm and then he grunted in satisfaction as he finished.

He lay his head down on my shoulder and we stayed perfectly still as our breathing slowed. When he looked up at me again it was Max's green eyes instead of Mr. Wolf's golden ones. "Achillia, I'm—"

I put my hand to his mouth and shook my head. "Don't apologize."

He started to pull away, and I moaned. He stopped moving and smiled. "Would you prefer me this time?"

I smiled. "You make it sound like I cheated on you."

He pushed into me, and my eyes rolled in the back of my head. He whispered, "Let me show you how it should have been." He carried me from the tub and into his bedroom. The silk sheets were cold on my back, but I soon forgot about everything around us. He kissed me and moved slowly, making the warmth build and build and build. I was ready to beg him to finish me when he bit into my neck, drawing blood and making me gasp. He released my neck then turned his head to the side. I didn't waste my opportunity as my body was already craving that last bit to push me over the edge. I bit into his neck, and the taste of his blood and increased movement from him, shoved me off the edge and drowned me. My body glowed bright red in my pleasure. I remembered to release his neck as he finished.

He stared down at me and smiled. "Better?"

I wasn't ready for words yet, so I simply nodded and licked the drops of his blood off of my lips. He laughed softly and gave me the first real smile I had seen in years. It lit up his entire face, and I smiled back at him. A pressure in my chest that had been building since Mr. Wolf had started this ordeal blossomed until it filled my entire body. Max's eyes were half gold and half green and I noticed the glowing light in the center of his chest. I watched in amazement as a thin wisp of gold pushed out of my chest at the same moment as one pushed out of Max's. The two pieces joined together and all of Max's memories, feelings, and thoughts rushed through my head like a slideshow. His happiness with his first mate, the children he had made, the sorrow and suicidal thoughts at his mate's loss, the battles he had won, the ones he had lost and the ones he had watched. The worry when he had found me and the love that had bloomed inside of him as I stayed with him and became part of the pack.

I wasn't sure how long it had taken, but when I looked back at Max I knew that he had seen a similar show from my head. Tears were leaking out of my eyes and I felt the drops from his. He had had a much longer show from my longer years. He kissed me and hugged me against him. "I love you, too, Achillia."

I stared at his worried face and whispered, "I'm sorry for the things you had to see, the things I had to do."

He shook his head. "I have always wanted to know what your life had been like before you met me and what you did when you were away on those trips. You're truly amazing."

I shook my head. "What about that battle in London? You killed two hundred other wolves by yourself? That was insane!"

He smiled. "You killed a dragon!"

I shrugged. "She wouldn't let me pass. I couldn't just let the warlock get away."

We laughed, and I found that even with Zack's death our mating had healed a part of me I hadn't known was broken. I was happy in a way I had not thought was possible. I had a moment of dizziness before I passed out to be sucked in to a dream with Eros.

Oh crap.

He stood before me, shining brightly, as he did when he was angry. I dropped to my hands and knees before him and held my tongue. He spoke quietly, "You have chosen."

I swallowed. "Yes."

He was very angry. Something broke nearby, and I waited in silence until he spoke to me again. "You are still mine."

I nodded. "I am still yours."

He sighed and the anger dissipated. "You will do my bidding before you do his. If you follow this rule, I will not strike the wolf down where he lays holding you."

I looked up and smiled. "I will do your bidding before his. My heart may belong to him, but my soul belongs to you my god, Eros. I am still your servant."

He smiled and touched my cheek softly. "You were never my servant and you know it. Defeat the bastard who harmed your wolf, and I will give you and your new mate a gift."

I dropped my head back down. "As you wish."

The dream dissipated as it had come and I was staring into Max's worried eyes. "Eros?"

I nodded. "Yes."

"Is he unhappy?" Max asked calmly.

"I am still his, in part, and will do his bidding and that is all he requires."

Max's face went neutral. "You are still his?"

I smiled. "You own my heart, but he owns my soul. I am your mate, but I am his servant."

Max relaxed his face and smiled. "I can agree to that. I do not like that you are not wholly mine, but I understand." His eyes flashed gold, and he shook his head regaining control. "He will understand it as well."

I frowned. "Am I the reason your control has been wavering?"

Max nodded. "Yes, but do not worry over it now. I am in control."

I kissed his lips and whispered, "The females are going to be devastated now. I'll have to fight a new challenge every day."

Max rolled his eyes. "That's different from every other day, how?"

I laughed. "Because now I really am alpha female."

Max tilted his head to the side in a very canine-like manner, which I had learned meant he was listening to someone nearby. "Luke wants to know if you're moving in here."

I frowned. "No. I need to stay..." The look on Max's face could have stopped a charging elephant in his tracks. "I mean... Yes."

Max smiled and kissed my cheek. "Good."

I sighed. "It feels wrong to be happy after what just happened."

Max nodded. "There will be time for mourning, but a mating is always a joyous event."

I laid my head on his chest. "Part of me is missing now. It'll never be healed."

Max rubbed my arm gently. "It will never be completely healed, but we can heal part of it. Zack wouldn't want you to mourn for him. He'd want you to kill the sonofabitch that did it to him."

I nodded. "I know."

Chapter 11

I stood on the porch of Max's house staring out at the trees. He'd summoned the pack earlier to advise them to prepare for battle and to send the children and the weakest women away. He now sat cross-legged in the middle of the porch, meditating. If the alpha could bring calmness to himself, he could bring calmness to his pack. Since I was not a werewolf of the pack, I was far from calm. I couldn't stop thinking about Zack, or about Richard. My grief was buried under my fury and desire for blood. Three knives, one long sword, one short sword, my two favorite axes, and five throwing daggers were attached to my outfitted body. All we had to do now was wait. Wait to see if Bryce would assist me. Wait to see if Richard brought another wolf pack into this battle. Wait to see who won and who died. I hated waiting.

"Stop that, Achillia." Max said calmly.

I looked down at him and frowned. "Stop what?"

He was within arm's reach of me and snatched my tail as it swept past him again. "Your tail is flickering everywhere and breaking my concentration."

I pulled my tail back from his hand and curled it around my leg. "My apologies. It has a mind of its own, especially when I'm distracted."

He shifted his weight and relaxed again. I didn't want him to fight because I worried he would die. He didn't want me to fight because he worried I would die. So, we came to a compromise, we both fought and neither of us could die. The sun began setting, casting a red glow over the compound that reminded me unsettlingly of blood. The moon rose into the night sky and glowed, half full. Wolves began walking from the tree line towards us and I noticed their attire. Every single wolf wore leather vests which covered their back, shoulders and stomach. Since they gained about two hundred pounds when they shifted to wolf form, they must have shifted while wearing the vests. That revelation made me ponder if it hurt to change into an abrasive material that touched their sensitive skin.

"It always hurts when we change, but you learn to harness the pain into anger and then to hold on to the anger for your fight," Max whispered.

I spun around and glared at him. "How did you—"

He opened his eyes and smiled. "Mate bond."

I hissed at him and felt my lips pull back over my fangs. "You bastard! You should have told me that we could have a mate bond!"

He stood slowly and shook as if flinging water from his body. "I wasn't sure that we could, since you are neither wolf nor human, but I'm telling you now." I wanted to be angry at him, but my anger was focused on the upcoming battle. Max wrapped his arms carefully around my waist, avoiding all of the silver objects I had strapped to me. "I love you, Achillia."

Just like that, four words and I was putty in his hands. "You're such a jerk." I whispered before I kissed his lips.

He smiled as he kissed me and said, "I'll take that as you love me, too."

I licked the tip of his nose and rubbed my cheek against his cheek, "I love you, too."

One of the wolves barked nearby, and I walked down the steps towards him. Luke lolled his tongue out the side of his mouth as I approached, and wagged his tail.

"Hey old friend, are you ready for one last battle?" My head only reached the top of his back, so I had to stand up on tiptoe to scratch his ears. He was the largest of the pack, a freak compared to the rest.

He barked, and then growled softly.

"'A few more battles,' is what he says," translated Max for me.

I patted the wolf on the head and walked to Max. He held up his hand and stripped his clothes off. I watched with increasing arousal, which made Max lift an eyebrow at me. I folded my arms across my chest and tried to look tough. Apparently, I failed because he smiled. His body shuddered and in a blink of an eye, a nine-foot-tall, half-man, half-wolf stood before me. He was the most beautiful creature I had ever seen and though I had seen it for more than two hundred years, it still took my breath away. I kept my eyes above his groin and smiled. Max began giving the normal pre-battle speech, but I couldn't focus on him anymore. I felt the magic users drawing near, making my skin crawl as though a thousand ants were running along me. I spread my wings and lifted up into the air, scouting for our enemies. A glint of metal caught my eye two miles away, and I whispered, "They are here."

The werewolves below me began yipping in that hunting song that drove humans into madness and brought anticipatory shivers to me. The wind stirred, and power began building around me, making my skin glow blue and the pupil of my eye disappeared. I could see clearer now and I looked at the army marching towards us. "Twenty warlocks, one hundred werewolves, and the leader who is a mix of warlock and wolf. The beta is in warrior form as you are, Max. The leader is mine." I said to the wolves below us.

Max growled softly, but I ignored him because he and I both knew he would be too busy fighting the beta of the werewolf pack to take down Richard. A fireball sizzled past my head and I laughed. "You missed, you cheap child's show magician!"

"Achillia," Max said calmly. I folded my wings in and dropped down to stand beside him.

He glared at me, and I shrugged. "Just having a bit of fun taunting them."

The first line of warlocks broke through the tree line, but they did not attack. I shook my hands loosely at my side as I prepared myself for the first strike. Knowing Richard, he would try to use an oxygen spell to make the werewolves believe they were suffocating, but I knew how to break it. Our enemies stood facing us, and I could see the hate on their faces, but knew it was mirrored on our faces as well. I gathered the raw magic between my hands and rolled it around between my fingers like a large ball. Max and I stood in front of our pack as we waited. Richard and the beta stepped in front of their group and Max growled as loud and long as he could. My eardrums were still ringing as the beta answered his challenge. Richard raised his hand and the oxygen spell descended upon us. The wolves around me never altered their positions as I spoke the incantation and shattered the spell. Richard glared at me and the beta wolf charged across the field towards us. Max ran out to meet him in a flurry of claws and teeth, and I pulled my swords from their sheaths. "The battle has begun."

I screamed my rage and sprinted across the field, hacking into the warlocks that now separated me from Richard. The bastard had retreated as soon as I had broken his spell. I slashed, stabbed, and hacked at the warlocks, cutting them down so that their spells died on their tongues with them. The sound of snarling, growling, screaming, and fighting made me deaf. I killed ten warlocks before my sword became too slick with their blood to hold anymore. I sheathed the swords and pulled my axes out, swinging them in a wide arc to take off two enemy wolves' heads as they jumped at me from each side. Their headless bodies fell to the ground beside me and I smiled at Richard. "So nice of you to run and hide behind your fodder. My blades were very hungry."

He smiled at me. "You think you can defeat me anymore than you could before? You will die by my blade this night, girl, just as surely as I killed your wolf."

I screamed and sliced at him. He dodged and parried my attacks with his sword. I continued to advance on him until I noticed the group of warlocks facing me and chanting. I dodged back from Richard and flew up into the air just as the warlocks released their spell. Fire spewed from their hands and Richard barely had time to form a shield to protect himself. Pulling three daggers from my belt, I chucked them into the backs of the warlocks and watched as they dropped face-forward on the ground.

I smiled. "You're a sneaky little shit, Richard. I would have never guessed that you knew you are weaker than me and set up a trap."

He growled, and his body shuddered into his warrior form. I heard Max howl in victory and turned to see him waving the head of the beta at the other wolves. Richard jumped into the air and grabbed at me. I slashed his stomach with my tail and folded my wings so that we fell at the same time. I attacked him with my sword, tail, and daggers. I wasn't fatally wounding him, but I was making hundreds of little cuts all over his body and pissing him off. My own body remained untouched and that seemed to set him over the edge. He pointed his palm at me and shoved. I flew backwards as his magic knocked me, landing on top of one of his wolves. She bit into my ankle. I screamed in pain and hacked off her head. Her jaws were still locked on my leg, but Richard ran torwards me so I had no time to pry it off. I sliced at him, but my ankle was bleeding a lot and my focus was wavering. I whispered urgently, "Ennio."

The tiger leapt from my arm and transformed into a giant beast of a feline. He roared and the bear leapt out after him, his roar shaking the ground. Max looked at me in shock and I smiled. "Attack them." The panther and bear didn't hesitate and began mauling the warlocks, who started to scream and flee in terror. The other pack began to come together to attack them, but Max barked an order and our pack kept them from working together. I only had a moment to smile happily, because Richard leapt at me and finished speaking his leeching spell as he hit me. My power began seeping away from me and into him, and I felt my energy draining. He slashed at me with his sword and I blocked his blows with my axe handles. He thrust forward faster than I could block and his sword pierced my left shoulder. I screamed in pain and he yanked the sword from me, thrusting again and piercing my right shoulder. I screamed again, but my vision was being covered by tiny black dots.

No, he couldn't win again. I couldn't let him win. I heard Max bellow in anger and felt him drawing closer to me. I knew I still had the extra power, but if I used it, Richard would just suck it up.

He bent down, pushing his sword deeper through my shoulder. "I thought you were going to give me a real challenge, girl. Do you want to know what your friend's last words were?" He didn't wait for me to finish and I couldn't focus on his face anymore. "They said he whispered your name as he died."

Richard stood, smiling smugly and raised his sword for his final blow. I didn't bother trying to protect myself and closed my eyes. I'd failed and now Max and his pack would suffer the consequences. Richard brought his sword down with a whistling sound, but a wind from above my head pushed his sword and him back. I opened my eyes and saw Bryce standing over me. "You shall not harm this girl."

Part of me wanted to laugh at the corny line and part of me wanted to jump up and kiss him. The only words that formed from my lips were, "You came."

Bryce knelt down and chanted quickly and quietly. The leeching spell shattered, and I could see clearly again, though my energy and magic were still gone. Richard howled in anger and ran forward, attacking Bryce. I watched as the boy matched his speed and agility easily and wondered where he had learned to fight.

Max appeared over me and changed completely to man. "Achillia, talk to me."

I whispered, "You're a pretentious, egotistical stubborn ass who is overprotective."

Max sighed. "Good, you're alright. Come on, let's get you up." I stood and Max kissed my forehead. "You aren't allowed to die on me. I thought we discussed this."

I giggled and looked up at his face. "I'm not dead yet." Ennio and the bear ran towards us and shrunk down as they jumped onto my body. I pulled up my shirt slowly, feeling blood gushing out of my shoulder wounds and pressed my belly button. Warmth radiated from my core, traveling up my chest to my shoulders and head and down my hips to my legs. My skin glowed brighter than ever, and my wounds closed instantly. I picked my axes up and smiled. "Time to finish this."

I ran forward and jumped between Richard and Bryce. Richard was caught off guard and I sliced his head off with my axes before he could mutter a single syllable of a spell. Max roared in victory, and I turned to Bryce.

"So, now what?" he asked me.

"You have to decide if you're going to help me open the gate. It is completely your decision and my pack will not harm you, no matter what you decide."

"I'll help you open the gate, but I need to recuperate some of my magic before I can do it. I'll meet you back here tomorrow night."

I hugged him and smiled happily up at him. "Thank you! You have no idea how happy you have made me!"

He smiled down at me and said, "You are very beautiful in this form. Can I touch your horns?"

I was about to say yes, but Max pulled me away.

"We're recently mated so he's a bit overprotective right now. Another day you may touch them," I explained.

"Only friends can touch her horns," Luke said from behind me, now in his man form.

"Bryce is my friend, right?" I asked him with a smile.

He smiled back and nodded. "Right. Okay, I'll see you tomorrow."

He walked away and it was then that I realized the battle was truly over. Bodies covered the ground around us and the scent of blood filled the air. "This is going to be a huge clean up job," I muttered.

Devon, one of the lower ranking wolves, had begun pouring a liquid substance on the dead bodies of our enemies. "It'll be quick actually," he told me. "We're just going to burn them."

"Did anyone from our pack get killed or seriously hurt?" I asked Max.

He shook his head. "No. The protection spells you placed on them all worked great." He then glared at me and said, "I would have preferred if you had used one on yourself."

I smiled and kissed him lightly. "I'm already healed so it would have been a waste."

"That boy is infatuated with you," Max said in a growl.

"I know. Sadly, I am already taken," I answered honestly.

Max hugged me and whispered, "And will be for the rest of eternity."

I let him take me into the house and to the bathroom where we spent quite a bit of time scrubbing dried blood off of each other. Max held me as we slept, and I felt content for the first time since coming to this world.

Chapter 12

I was surprised not to have been visited by Eros, but supposed that was because we would see each other in person soon. What would those at Olympus think of this world? What would they think of my pack? Would my old friends be able to interact with them?

What would Ares think? Or Apollo? Or Heracles?

I blew out a deep breath and tried to calm down. Everything would be fine. No matter what happened I was Max's now.

"Hello," Bryce said pleasantly from in front of me.

My head jerked up since I had not heard him come up. "Hi."

"Sorry, I didn't mean to startle you."

"It's okay," I said and smiled warmly at him.

Max walked out and extended his hand to Bryce. "Bryce."

Bryce blinked at him, but shook his hand. "Max."

"Are you recuperated enough to perform this spell?" Max asked him.

Bryce nodded. "Yes, but mainly because she will be helping me."

"So, where's the gate?" I asked him.

He smirked and said, "Follow me."

Max and I exchanged glances and then followed him as he walked towards the center of the area we had battled in yesterday. "I wasn't sure this was it," he told us over his shoulder. "But during the battle I felt it and knew for certain it was here." He stopped and traced a large rectangle in front of him and it glowed brightly.

I stepped forward and touched the place I had been over a hundred dozen times. "How did I miss it?" I asked softly.

"You probably didn't think to look here," Bryce whispered.

He was right. I hadn't thought to look at the pack's territory. Maybe that's why I had been drawn here? Maybe that's why the pack was here?

"So, let's get this show started," I said eagerly.

He put his hands against the glowing rectangle and closed his eyes. Light pulsed from his hands into the rectangle with each breath. "Come help me," he whispered.

I kissed Max's cheek and then placed my hands on either side of Bryce's. It was finally happening. I would finally fulfill my goal. I took a deep breath and added my magic to his. I could feel the spell unraveling and it made me smile. We were so close.

The web of the spell slowly came apart and with a loud explosion the doorway opened. Bryce and I were thrown backwards, but Max caught us before we hit the ground.

"Achillia!" he yelled at me.

"I'm okay, just tired," I whispered as I opened my eyes. The sky had turned a light purple color and I watched victoriously as Mount Olympus came into view.

A golden chariot pulled by pegasi raced across the sky and then landed in front of us. Apollo leapt from his chariot and raced towards me with an ear-splitting smile. He took me from Max's arms and spun me around while hugging me. "You beautiful, perfect woman! You did it! I knew you would!" He planted a huge kiss on my lips and then set me down.

I beamed proudly at him and tried to ignore the kiss he had just given me. "Thank you, Apollo. I wouldn't have been able to do it without my friends' help though."

He turned and looked at the two men behind me and said, "You chose wisely when picking friends, Achillia."

Max dropped to one knee and bowed. "Apollo."

Apollo said, "You did well protecting her, Max."

"Achillia!" a male voice shouted happily. Heracles, Eros, and Ares landed on the grass in front of me and before I could object I was passed around for hugs.

Ares held me at arm's length and said, "Well done. You have made me immensely proud."

I blushed and said, "Thanks."

He smirked at me and then looked at Max. "Who is this?"

Max's jaw was clenched, and I could see the anger brewing in his eyes. I took a step back and linked hands with Max. "This, is Max, alpha of the Western Valley Pack and my husband."

"Your what!?" Apollo and Heracles yelled at the same time.

Max glanced at me and said, "I prefer the term mate."

"Have you been married?" Apollo asked, crossing his arms over his chest.

"Not in the way you're assuming, but we are mated and it's far more binding than a basic wedding ceremony," Max answered.

Eros waved his hand at us. "Can't you see the link between them?" he asked Apollo.

Apollo squinted and then frowned deeply. "This is highly unfortunate."

"Why is that?" I asked nervously.

"I had planned to make you my queen."

"She's my servant. You never discussed it with me," Eros said between his teeth.

"She's her own person," Apollo snapped.

"Children," Ares said and pinched the bridge of his nose. "Let's stop this bickering. We are here to celebrate, and you're giving our audience a terrible first impression."

Heracles walked around Max and me slowly and asked, "What are your fighting abilities?"

"Hey!" I snapped at all of the gods, making them turn to look at me. "Leave him alone. You can have a pissing contest later, but not now."

"She's even sexier than before," Heracles said with a smirk.

I drew my sword and pointed it at him. "Enough. Stop trying to rile him up for a fight."

He whispered, "You're choosing him over a god. You realize that, right?"

"I love him," I stated simply.

Apollo ground his teeth together and said, "I told you to protect her, not take her."

Max lifted my hand to kiss my knuckles and said, "Try as I might, I couldn't resist the spell she put me under."

"Eros, I believe you have something to tell her," Ares said.

Eros sighed. "Well, you've obviously chosen your suitor. And I imagine you have chosen to stay here instead of returning to Mount Olympus with us."

"Yes."

"And as of this moment you are no longer my servant, not that you truly were before," Eros said, muttering the last part under his breath.

"Thank you."

"What of your final boon?" Eros asked.

I'd been thinking about this for a while, and I still wasn't completely sure. I could ask to be able to have kids, but Max didn't seem like he wanted more kids. I did have one other option.

"Is there a way that I could stop aging without consuming souls for Hades anymore?" I asked softly.

"I don't care if you age," Max told me.

I smiled at him and said, "I know, Max, but you age slower than normal and I don't want to look like an old hag while you still look like this."

"You'd be just as beautiful to me," he whispered.

I nuzzled his shoulder and turned back to Eros. "Please."

"That is not my decision, but I can request it and—"

"That is my decision," Hades said as he materialized in front of me.

I bowed my head. "Hades."

He smiled. "Achillia, in appreciation for opening the door and for the large number of souls you sent me, I will grant you your wish."

"Really?" My eyes widened. I hadn't thought it would be so easy.

"Step away from your mate and close your eyes," Hades ordered me.

"Will this hurt her?" Max asked as he reluctantly let go of my hand.

"Oh, yes," Hades said with a wicked smile. I closed my eyes, and he put a hand on my mouth and one on my sternum just as he had done when I first left. Pain engulfed me and despite my attempts, I screamed.

I could hear Max growling and hear Apollo speaking to him. Finally, the pain eased, and I could open my eyes. I felt weird, but good. "Thank you," I whispered.

"You still have a boon," Ares said.

I looked back up at Hades and he sighed. "You ask much of me, girl."

"Please, Hades. I will do whatever you ask of me. Please, just one more thing," I begged him.

He stared at me a moment and then said, "Don't let it be known that the God of Death is merciful at times."

He snapped his fingers and Zack appeared in front of us, whole and healthy. He looked at his hands and body and asked, "What happened?"

"What?" Max asked in shock.

I leapt onto Zack, knocking him to the ground and hugged him tightly. "I love you, brother."

Zack hugged me tightly and said, "I love you too, sister. Why are you crying?"

I sniffed and wiped my tears off on my shirt. "You died for a bit, but you're fine now."

"I don't remember dying."

"Good," I said adamantly and rubbed my face against his.

Max pulled us up and embraced Zack warmly. "It's good to have you back."

"We are off to begin our work," Ares said, drawing my attention back to them.

I turned and dropped to my knees, bowing until my forehead touched the ground. "Thank you."

Ares pulled me up and said, "From this day forward, you bow to no one."

I smiled at him and then stepped back next to Max and Zack. Ares disappeared and one after another, the other gods disappeared until it was only Apollo left. He stood in front of us with a scowl. "After today, I won't visit you again," he said softly.

I had known he would feel this way, but seeing him and the sadness my decision had caused him made me feel like a teenager again. "I'm sorry, Apollo."

He looked up at me and said, "You'll always be in my heart, Achillia. As much as I should forget you, I know I won't be able to." He walked forward and stopped just out of my reach. I stepped away from Max and Apollo hugged me tightly. He whispered into my ear, "If you're ever in trouble you may call upon me. I love you, Achillia."

He disappeared and sunshine warmed my lips as he kissed me while leaving.

Max growled angrily behind me and said, "He's lucky he is a god."

I turned and smiled at him. "You should be careful. They might start testing you, if you show no fear."

"I'm not afraid of them."

I kissed his cheek and said, "And that is part of why I love you."

"Wait, what happened between you two?" Zack asked in shock. "Are you mated?"

"Yes," I said with a smile to him.

He picked me up and spun me around. "It's about time!"

* * *

Most of the humans were resistant to the gods at first, but some immediately came to the gods for protection. The military tried to resist as well, but that was pointless. The gods were truly immortal and could not be killed, so their tanks and missiles had no effect. Especially, when Aphrodite turned a fleet of tanks into a herd of pegasi.

Our pack was given full protection, magical borders were erected to keep intruders out, and we experienced true peace for the first time in hundreds of years.

Life wasn't perfect. Bad things still happened, but the gods cured cancer, ended hunger, and put the homeless to work in their temples.

I didn't know what the next two hundred years would bring, but with Max as my mate, and Zack by my side, I knew we could accomplish anything.

THANKS FOR READING!

Website
www.CatherineBanks.com

Newsletter
http://catbanks.co/newsletter

ABOUT THE AUTHOR

Catherine Banks is a USA Today bestselling fantasy author who writes in several fantasy subgenres under two pseudonyms. She began writing fiction at only four years old and finished her first full-length novel at the age of fifteen. She is married to her soulmate and best friend, Avery, who she has two amazing children with. After her full-time job, she reads books, plays video games, and watches anime shows and movies with her family to relax. Although she has lived in Northern California her entire life, she dreams of traveling around the world. Catherine is also C.E.O. of Turbo Kitten Industries™, a company with many hats including being a book publisher and Etsy store full of nerdy fun.

facebook.com/CatherineBanksAuthor

twitter.com/catherineebanks

ALSO BY CATHERINE BANKS

Song of the Moon (Artemis Lupine, Book One)

Kiss of a Star (Artemis Lupine, Book Two)

Healed by Fire (Artemis Lupine, Book Three)

Taming Darkness (Artemis Lupine, Book Four)

ARTEMIS LUPINE THE COMPLETE SERIES (Books 1-4)

Pirate Princess (Pirate Princess, Book One)

Princess Triumvirate (Pirate Princess, Book Two)

Mercenary (Little Death Bringer, Book One)

Protector (Little Death Bringer, Book Two)

Royally Entangled (Her Royal Harem, Book One)

Royally Exposed (Her Royal Harem, Book Two)

Royally Elected (Her Royal Harem, Book Three)

Royally Enraged (Her Royal Harem, Book Four)

True Faces (Ciara Steele Novella, #1)

Barbaric Tendencies (Ciara Steele Novella, #2)

Demonic Contract (Dragon Kissed Trilogy, Book One)

Anja's Secret (Anja of Plisnar, Book One)

Daughter of Lions

Centaur's Prize

Dragon's Blood

The Last Werewolf

Bitten, Beaten, & Loved

Also by Catherine Banks

Lady Serra and the Draconian

Last Ama Princess

Alys of Asgard

Tiger Tears

Calvin's Alien Adventure

Sybil Deceived

Olansia

The Pawn

CONNECT WITH CATHERINE BANKS

I really appreciate you reading my book! Here are some ways to connect with me:

Website:

www.catherinebanks.com

Follow me on BookBub:

https://www.bookbub.com/authors/catherine-banks

Join my newsletter for deals and snippets:

http://catbanks.co/newsletter

Like my author Facebook page:

http://www.Facebook.com/CatherineBanksAuthor

Follow me on Twitter:

http://www.Twitter.com/catherineebanks

Follow me on Goodreads:

http://www.Goodreads.com/catherine_banks

www.ingramcontent.com/pod-product-compliance
Lightning Source LLC
Chambersburg PA
CBHW050752250626
47155CB00005B/2035